TALES OF
SUBURBAN
CASTAWAYS
& OTHER STORIES

Cover design: Lídia Puccetti | lidiapuccetti.com
Front cover image (angel): Lídia Puccetti / Midjourney
Back cover image (butterfly, brick wall): Lídia Puccetti / Midjourney
Interior line art (suitcases, butterfly, wings): Bel Vidal / Magic Media™

ISBN 978-0-6458661-2-4 (paperback)
ISBN 978-0-6458661-3-1 (eBook)

Printed in Australia. Typeset in Montserrat 10.5

Part 1 depicts real events and people - some names have been changed. All characters and situations in Parts 2 and 3 are fictional.

A catalogue record for this book is available from the National Library of Australia

TALES OF SUBURBAN CASTAWAYS

& OTHER STORIES

BEL VIDAL

About the Author

Bel Vidal is the pen name of a Bolivian-born writer who has called Sydney home since 1988.

Her works of fiction, non-fiction and poetry have been widely published, both in English and Spanish, under her pen name, her real name, and other pseudonyms. She was the recipient of an Australian Council of the Arts grant to publish a bilingual collection of poems and short stories, *Arcoiris de Sueños/Rainbow of Dreams* (Cervantes Publishing, 1993).

An early draft of Bel's debut novel, *Exuberance*, was shortlisted for the Varuna-Harper Collins award for manuscript development, and was awarded the five-day Varuna Awards Residential Masterclass. *Exuberance* was independently published in 2023.

Bel is employed as a communications specialist in the not-for-profit sector. Outside work, she is a mental health advocate, book and art lover, film buff, hiker, traveller, blogger, and firm believer it is never too late to start something new.

Find out more at **belvidal.com**

Contents

PART 1:
IN TRANSIT
SELECTED NON-FICTION

The First Australian

He was not a hero or a celebrity, just an ordinary man who died in extraordinary circumstances. You would have seen his face on the front page of the papers back in September 2001, a close-up of a gentle-looking man in his 60s, smiling from ear to ear, wearing glasses and a baseball cap. The face of Alberto Dominguez, the first Australian to die in the September 11 terrorist attacks. Dominguez had delayed his trip back from Boston by a day and was aboard American Airlines flight 11 when it ploughed onto the northern tower of the World Trade Centre on the day we will never forget.

I didn't know Dominguez when he was alive, but I came to learn a lot about him after his death. As an immigrant of similar ethnic background, I took particular interest in his story; more specifically, in the part of his story that did not reach the Australian public.

What you would have heard about Dominguez through the media reports was that he was a Uruguayan-born migrant, father of four, who worked as a baggage handler for Qantas. In most of the many media profiles that followed the attacks, Dominguez's identity was defined by what he did for a living: a 'baggie', evidently much loved among his colleagues, who all donated a day's pay after the tragedy, raising A$18,000 for his family. However, the reports were not only incomplete, but also often inaccurate. In one, his wife was referred to as Myrna, not Martha (Myrna was Martha's sister, whom they had gone to visit in Boston); in another, he was said to have worked at Qantas for 21 years, when in fact he was just about to complete his tenth year with the company. All in all, apart from learning that 'he was a very gentle man who loved a joke', we were left with only a little more knowledge about this man than the men who'd killed him had.

The news coverage on ABC Radio offered a glimpse into a different dimension of Dominguez's life, reporting that he had 'pioneered Spanish-language radio in Australia'. This prompted my co-workers to ask me whether I knew him, as they were aware that Spanish was my mother tongue. At the time I had to answer in the negative; I am one of those immigrants who, in their effort to assimilate, did not maintain ties to their ethnic community.

However, I could still read and understand Spanish, and it didn't take me long to find out, by consulting the Spanish-language press, that Alberto Dominguez (nicknamed 'Pocho') was a household name among the members of his community. He had worked for Special Broadcasting Service (SBS) radio for 13 years, since its inception as Radio Ethnic Australia in 1975. When over 40,000 Latin American migrants arrived in Australia in the late 1970s and early 1980s, Dominguez's voice was one of the first friendly voices they heard, welcoming them to their new home in a language they could understand, and providing vital information that assisted them in the process of settling.

'Pocho' was also remembered as one of the founding members of the Uruguayan Club; the United Uruguayans; the Association of Spanish-Speaking Grandparents; and the Latin American Relief Foundation.

When I looked at the list of casualties by country, I noticed there was another Alberto Dominguez of the same age, listed under the Uruguayan casualties as a 'former cycling champion'. A quick search through *La República*, an online Uruguayan paper, confirmed that they were in fact the same man. In 1953, long before he left Uruguay to come to Australia, Dominguez had won that country's national speed-cycling championship. He had been part of the Uruguayan Olympic cycling team in 1957, and also represented Uruguay in the Pan-American games in Chicago in 1959, and in São Paulo in 1963.

It is said that in the act of migration we suffer the metaphorical death of our previous identity. We need to re-invent ourselves, and are often reincarnated as different people, with different occupations, pre-occupations and priorities. Thus, the former cycling champion/electrician became a radio broadcaster/baggage handler in his adopted country.

In Australia, like many other migrants, Alberto Dominguez led a dual life. In one life he was a prominent member of the Spanish community, and in another he was the migrant worker who could not speak fluent English. He developed a bifurcated identity; the 'persona' he was in private, among family and compatriots, was completely different from the 'public entity' that integrated into the mainstream. The first one, 'Pocho', was more assertive, having retained most of the characteristics from his former life, whilst the second one, 'Albert', was less defined. Albert's co-workers at Qantas described him as a 'very gentle man', whereas his Uruguayan cycling coach and his friends in the South American community remembered Pocho as strong willed and hot tempered.

There is another metaphor often used in studies of migration. The concept of migrants becoming 'lost in translation' has been immortalised by Eva Hoffman in her autobiography of the same name (Vintage, 1998). In my view, this is what happened to Alberto 'Pocho' Dominguez. His achievements as a man who found realisation in an English-speaking country, by using a language other than English to make a contribution and to bring a service to the community, were considered of no relevance to mainstream Australia. As a consequence, Dominguez's two parallel lives became completely disassociated from each other after his death, and one of them all but vanished in the process of translation.

It seems a pity that Dominguez stepped into Australian history merely as the migrant who 'spent the last years of his life handling baggage marked "fragile"' because the media were selective in their reports. It occurred to me that I could use my bilingual skills to rescue the pieces of Dominguez's – or rather, Pocho's – life that did not transcend beyond the limits of his community and, at the same time, attempt to place this community in the Australian cultural mosaic.

A few months after Pocho's death, I found myself in front of a microphone at Radio Austral, a Spanish-language radio station based in Fairfield, on air with Eduardo Gonzales,

Austral's director, discussing Pocho's life. With Pocho's family's consent, I had made Pocho the subject of my master's research project. Gonzales had also been one of the pioneers of Spanish-language broadcasting and he invited me to speak on Austral.

One of the people who called me after the program was Mrs Norma Méndez, a seamstress who worked in Pitt Street. She had recorded most of the programs Pocho produced in the years that SBS was the only radio station in Australia broadcasting in Spanish. Mrs Méndez was willing to lend me her precious collection of tapes for as long as I needed it, on the condition I returned it intact.

'He was a member of my family, although we never met in person,' Norma told me when I called in at her workshop to collect the box of tapes. 'We often spoke on the phone; I was always calling his program. The day he left SBS was a very sad day for him and all his listeners.' As one does when a member of the family dies, Mrs Méndez closed her workshop on 26 September 2001 to attend Pocho's memorial service at St Andrew's Cathedral. She found it packed; apart from his family and dozens of his Qantas colleagues, hundreds of members of the Spanish-speaking community had travelled from all corners of Sydney to be there.

The experience of immersing myself in Pocho's life involved taking a journey back to my origins and back in time, as I listened to recordings of programs that were aired when I was a child still living in Bolivia, and revisited the music and the language I grew up with. Pocho loved to play tangos and boleros; in fact, he was best remembered for his program *Folklore, Tangos y Rosas*. And as most South Americans do, he also had a passion for *fútbol* (soccer).

This journey also reconnected me with the South American community and with people I hadn't seen for over a decade. I was amazed that whenever I mentioned Pocho's name among them, there was always someone who knew him and wanted to contribute with a minor or major detail, or give me a lead for my research.

Among Norma's tapes was one that was dated 15 July 1988 and labelled *Adios del Pocho* – 'Pocho's goodbye'. That was the date of my twentieth birthday, the very first birthday I spent in Australia. It was also the day Pocho ended his 13-year association with SBS, having fallen under the axe of 'corporate restructure'. Whilst he cried on air as all his friends and colleagues turned up at the studio to farewell him, I was crying on a ferry on my way to Taronga Zoo, thinking of all the friends I had left behind in Bolivia who weren't around to celebrate my birthday with me.

These tapes also reacquainted me with events that were taking place in 1988, the year that I came to live in Australia; the Australian Bicentenary. I had missed the significance of these celebrations because I was still trying to make sense of my new surroundings and finding my place in this society.

On this farewell program, Pocho's voice, which was usually smooth and pleasant, sounded rather coarse. This was not only because he was on the verge of tears, but also because the previous night he had gone to see the final of the Bicentennial Gold Cup of Soccer. He had spent most of the Australia versus Argentina game screaming at the top of his lungs. He confessed he had divided loyalties, but admitted that Australia deserved to win the match (the score was 4–1) and that the Australian team had come a long way to defeat the former world champions.

Shortly after my meeting with Norma, I was contacted by two of Pocho's close friends, Néstor Alzamendi and Rubén Fernández-Ferro. They had both known Pocho since their arrival in Australia in the 1970s, and had also worked with him in community radio. Prior to his fateful trip to Boston, Pocho was co-hosting a weekly program, *Entre Amigos (Between Friends)* on radio B FM in Bankstown with Alzamendi; and Fernández-Ferro had taken Pocho's place while he travelled to America with his wife. They were visiting Martha's sister, Myrna. She was receiving specialist treatment for a brain tumour in Boston, where she lived.

From our conversations, it transpired that Pocho had continued his work in community radio after leaving SBS. He worked on a voluntary basis, often paying for the air space out of his own pocket, on 2SER, 2GLF, B FM and Radio Rio. He had been planning to volunteer on a full-time basis at Radio Austral after his retirement from Qantas, which was due to happen just weeks after he died.

Pocho also organised literary competitions and soccer championships. He contributed regularly to the newspaper *Noticias y Deportes (News and Sport)* and he even had a brief stint as a community television host on Channel 31. In 1998, when Hurricane Mitch devastated Belize, Nicaragua, El Salvador, Honduras and Guatemala, he established the Latin American Relief Foundation, which continued to operate afterwards to raise funds for other Latin American countries struck by natural disasters. He did all this, his friends said, while holding a full-time job and spending quality time with his wife, four children and six grandchildren.

Alzamendi also brought me a tape. It was the recording

of a program he produced in 2000 as a surprise to Pocho, commemorating Pocho's twenty-fifth anniversary as a radio broadcaster in Australia. Throughout the program, Pocho emotionally reminisces about his 13 years at SBS and, in particular, about one of the few occasions when the South American community took centre stage in the streets of Sydney:

> *When Argentina won the world cup in 1978... it was madness – I thought I'd be taken to jail! During the program I invited the audience to come and join us at our studio in Clarence Street to celebrate. I never expected that hundreds of them would turn up. They brought flags, and were singing and dancing in the street. The police came and wanted to know who was responsible for this unauthorised demonstration, and the manager of the radio, who used to call me 'Poncho', asked, 'What do we do now?' The only thing I could think of was to install two speakers outside for the crowd to hear the program live. Afterwards, even the police joined in, and escorted over one thousand South Americans as they triumphantly marched to Martin Place. Rodolfo Rivarola, president of the Argentine Association at the time, took responsibility for the entire thing and saved my life. It was exhilarating.*

'It was an incredible experience,' said Alzamendi, with tears in his eyes. 'Nothing like that has ever happened again, and probably never will, because things have changed a lot here in Australia.'

Perhaps what happened to Pocho's identity in the aftermath of September 11 is a reflection of how much 'things have changed' in Australia since the time of his arrival.

The Dominguez family arrived in 1972, when Australia's

immigration policy was shifting away from the assimilationist tendencies that characterised the post-war years. Winning the 'ethnic vote' had become important, and migrants from non-English-speaking backgrounds were suddenly visible in the political scene. Ethnic affairs advisory councils were formed, ethnic groups received funding to help them settle while maintaining their cultural heritage, and the idea of multiculturalism was born.

Al Grasby, notorious for his support of multiculturalism, noted in his book *The Spanish in Australia* (AE Press, 1983) that ethnic radio was crucial for the development of Australia as a multicultural society, contributing towards 'the building of tolerance and understanding, and a new program to enable English-speaking Australians to break out of monolingual and monocultural boxes.'

Radio Ethnic Australia was launched by Al Grasby in June 1975. It began as a pilot program, aiming to provide information about health services and a lifeline to non-Anglophone migrants, who in Grasby's own words were 'the ignored and silent millions, mostly workers who bent their backs in tough jobs to keep the nation running'.

The ethnic radio experiment started with a budget of $49,000 and initially went on air in seven languages in Sydney (2EA), including Spanish, and eight languages in Melbourne (3EA). In 1976, the Fraser government set up SBS to run the EA stations.

Grasby enlisted the help of three full-time staff for both cities, and approximately 100 unpaid volunteers who spoke community languages. Pocho was among those volunteers, and later he would become a contractor.

Gillian Bottomley says, in her book *From another place*:

migration and the politics of culture (Cambridge University Press, 1992), that 'many of the struggles over adjustment in a new society are struggles over language, sometimes for basic understanding, sometimes for recognition.' Bottomley goes on to say that in Australia, the policy of multiculturalism helped minorities obtain some of that recognition, particularly when community languages were given an official status.

In the decades since its inception, SBS radio has continued to grow and now broadcasts in 68 languages, but the ideal behind its creation has long fallen out of favour. The demise of multiculturalism began in 1988, in the aftermath of the Fitzgerald report, which found that:

> *Multiculturalism has come to be seen as something for immigrants and ethnic communities only, and not for the whole of Australia. Aboriginals, for example, have not wanted to identify with it. Many other older generation Australians believe it has nothing to do with them.*

By the time Pocho died in 2001, multiculturalism had been dismantled as a national policy by the Howard government. Nowadays, according to research by Associate Professor Jim Forrest of Macquarie University and Dr Kevin Dunn of the University of New South Wales, Australia is gradually returning to being the ethnocultural nation it was in the 1950s, where migrants from diverse cultural backgrounds 'are expected to assimilate into the dominant Anglo-Celtic culture.'

Another explanation for the fact that Pocho Dominguez's achievements did not transcend into the mainstream could be that the Dominguez family did not completely assimilate into Australia's dominant, English-speaking culture. For all practical purposes they had integrated well into Australian society (in other words they held jobs, paid their taxes, became law-abiding Australian citizens and pursued, among other common goals, the 'great Australian dream' of owning a house in the suburbs), but their private lives and social activities revolved around people who spoke their own language.

This could have less to do with a deliberate choice than the fact that their first months in Sydney were spent at the Villawood Migrant Hostel, which back in the early 1970s was populated by South American migrants. Pocho's daughter, Virginia, who was 13 when they arrived, told me it didn't feel as if they had emigrated at all because a big chunk of South America had been transported with them to the other side of the world.

In contrast to the post-war migrants who were dispersed to remote camps, and today's refugees who spend months and even years in detention centres, the South American migrants who arrived in the 1970s hold cherished memories of their migrant hostel days. Most of them were fleeing countries in economic and political turmoil, and found themselves welcomed with open arms by a host society that provided them with a structure of support from the moment they arrived. Being able to form connections in the hostel among other Spanish-speakers also helped them minimise the trauma of immigration.

Since language is so closely associated with cultural identity, it is not surprising that the majority of the above South American migrants settled in the surrounding areas of Villawood, Carramar and Fairfield, where they could maintain the life-long friendships they had formed at the hostel among people who spoke their mother tongue.

Both Pocho and Martha were allocated jobs within days of arriving and they didn't stay long at the hostel. They moved to a fully equipped government housing flat in Auburn (Martha recalled that it even had cutlery in the kitchen drawers) and eventually bought a house in Lidcombe, but they never lost their ties with the Spanish-speaking community.

The Dominguez family, either by choice or by circumstance, fell into the category of migrants who tend to hold onto their cultural identities. But even if they had actively tried to assimilate... is such a thing as a 'complete' assimilation possible for first generation migrants who come from a different culture and speak a different language?

My brother and I, for instance, fall into the second category of migrants. We were 14 and 19 respectively when we arrived in 1988, and decided early on that we had not uprooted ourselves and shifted to the other side of the world only to replicate the world we had come from. As Paul White says in *Writing across worlds: literature and migration* (Routledge, 1995), 'why migrate if such movement does not result in change, or does not accommodate an identity change that has already occurred?'

The process has taken a long time – longer for me than for my brother, who was still of school age when we arrived – but we both managed to learn English, acquire advanced degrees at university, find well-remunerated professional jobs in our fields, and form an Anglophone circle of friends and relations. Although we still have a foreign accent, a foreign appearance and a foreign name, we have reached a stage where our skills, qualifications and fluency in English warrant us the same career and social opportunities as any other Australian.

In the act of assimilation, we have lost important aspects of our cultural identity, but we have also discovered there are many other dimensions to this identity that, along with our accent and our appearance, cannot be discarded or replaced. My interest in Pocho's story, for instance, reflects the unbreakable bond that ties me to my beginnings.

My brother and I will always remain migrants, both subjectively and in the eyes of others, regardless of how willing we have been to assimilate or how embracing this society has been towards us. This proves that the process of assimilation is much more complex than simply expecting that ethnic groups will give up what they brought with them to blend into the mainstream.

Nevertheless, being able to 'blend in' to the point that we have, has brought us many rewards; among them a level of professional recognition and visibility that we would have not achieved within the confines of the Spanish-speaking circle, a community that (like most non-Anglophone minorities) has always remained on the periphery of Australian society.

This community's invisibility is exacerbated both by its small size and by the fact that Spanish-speaking migrants don't call attention to themselves, as they have integrated into Australian society fairly smoothly.

Seeing the extent to which Pocho's achievements were overlooked by the mainstream press, prompted me to ask his wife, Martha, whether he ever expressed frustration at the invisibility that came with being a Spanish speaker in Australia.

She answered me with conviction: 'There is something I want to make sure you highlight when you write about him,' she said, emphasising each word. 'Pocho was very happy here. He had what he wanted the most: a decent job to provide for his family; something that was becoming increasingly difficult in Uruguay.'

Martha's words brought to my mind a scene in Eva Hoffman's autobiography, *Lost in Translation* (Vintage, 1998). Hoffman was a Polish migrant who settled in New York and eventually became editor of the *New York Times Book Review* and an acclaimed author. In this particular scene, she describes a conversation with her Brazilian cleaning lady, Maria, who is having trouble feeding herself and her daughter, but is determined to bring her son and his family to America as well.

She asks Maria why her son, who has an engineering degree in Brazil, would want to move to New York. He would have little chance of finding a job in his field, and might also end up working as a cleaner. Maria puts things into perspective for her, explaining that in Brazil he often can't feed his family. They don't even have hot water. In New York, he can at least have a hot shower after work, whatever he ends up doing. Although she understands that for people such as Maria and her son, the point of migration is mainly to have a better life, Hoffman is still trying to learn to live with a 'bifurcated identity'.

Before I started my quest to salvage Pocho Dominguez's memory from oblivion, I had assumed most migrants would be like Hoffman and me, for whom the urge to transcend into the mainstream of our adopted country can become both a motivation and a curse; for whom learning the new language to the best of our abilities is paramount; for whom living a comfortable, quiet life in better conditions than we would have had in our native countries is not sufficient.

What I learned about Pocho's life through the testimonies of his friends and members of his family has challenged each one of my assumptions. Rubén Fernández-Ferro said that Pocho considered himself *un Australiano de habla hispana* - a 'Spanish-speaking Australian', and as such, he found realisation and the means to make a significant contribution to Australian society without the need to break the language barrier. It is a credit to this society that it allowed him to feel *Australiano* without having to give up his cultural identity and the use of his mother tongue. As long as Dominguez could have a decent job and provide for his family, it did not matter to him whether his other achievements transcended into mainstream Australia; at least not to the extent it seems to matter to me.

Nevertheless, I still maintain that if this man entered national history as the first Australian to die in the September 11 World Trade Centre attacks, a more complete portrait of his character and achievements should have been painted, and this should have included his accomplishments as a sportsman and details of the life he led as a 'Spanish-speaking Australian'. A man who made a considerable impact within a community that, although largely unnoticed, is still a part of Australia's culturally diverse society and history.

One of the mainstream media articles that appeared following Pocho's death reported that the Dominguez family were struggling to put Pocho's life into words because there seemed to be 'too much to summarise'. I am sure the reporters who had in their hands the power to write the official version of history could have helped Pocho's family to find those words. At least I can now say, I have tried.

This essay was the opening piece of *Culture is... Australian Stories Across Cultures*, an anthology edited by Anne-Marie Smith (Wakefield Press, 2008). The anthology, published in association with The Multicultural Writers Association of Australia, was shortlisted for a Human Rights Award in Literature – Non-Fiction in 2009.

The Tunnel

You are the writer. No, you're the fountain pen in the writer's hand, the blue ink flowing on white paper, tracing a path of language into the unknown.

When reflecting on poetic creation in his essay 'The Rhythm', Octavio Paz says: 'language, like the universe, is a world of callings and answers, ebb and flow, unity and separation, inspiration and expiration.'[1]

You walk along this winding path. It seems to ebb and flow incessantly, creating itself as you walk over it. And you can smell the fragrance of grass, damp after the rain. You can hear the singing of birds at dawn. Yet you see nothing, for it is completely dark. All you can distinguish is a faint light at the end of a tunnel.

One of my favourite Latin American authors, Jorge Luis Borges, is obsessed with labyrinths and mirrors, among other literary images. One of my obsessions, apart from Borges, is tunnels.

---

1 Paz, Octavio 'The Rhythm' in *The Bow and the Lyre* (El Arco y la Lira), Fondo de Cultura Económica, Mexico, 1956. Translated from the original Spanish.

ය

The notion of a tunnel as a path into the unknown is intriguing. They have the power to take you from one space to another. Even a lift is a tunnel. You get on it at a certain floor, and when the doors open you find yourself in a completely different space.

In the city, sometimes you take the lift in one of those ultra-modern buildings with glass and mirror walls. You can hit the wrong button in the elevator and all of a sudden, the doors open and you step into an unfamiliar floor, ghostly and deserted. The walls and carpets have been ripped apart, slabs of concrete are thrown here and there, the smell of construction fills your lungs. There is a sense of disruption about this refurbishing – it creates an alien, barbaric space suspended in the middle of civilisation. You quickly get back into the safety of your vertical tunnel and, with a shaky finger, find the right button.

Worm holes are also tunnels. They take you from one dimension to another. Whether I intend it or not, tunnels always pop up in my writing.

ය

You walk inside the Devonshire Street underground tunnel at Central Station, obeying the traffic rules: always walk on the left unless overtaking. The murals on the walls seem to recycle themselves, like the scrolling backdrops in old theatre plays, while a stream of faceless people ebbs and flows in both directions, resembling zombies. You notice they never look you in the eyes. You observe more carefully, and realise they never look anybody in the eyes. Everybody walks with their gaze fixed on some point lost in space.

You think this must have something to do with the Anglo-Saxon character. In South America, men not only look you in the eyes, but many virtually undress you with their gaze and make catcall-like comments about your appearance as they pass by. They call that *piropos*.

> piropo – *pronounced pee-ró-po (the* Collins Spanish-English Dictionary*): [1] Amorous compliment, flirtatious [2] garnet, ruby [3] ticking off.*

Definition [1] is a very mild definition for what a *piropo* is. This word is one of those untranslatable expressions that has to be experienced in order to be understood. *Piropos* are not only a part of Latin-American culture, they also are a form of art. *'El arte de piropear'*, like any other art, can also have its deviations: it can be very gallant and tasteful, but sometimes it can be rude, offensive and even physical, depending on the degree of education or social status of the male.

The way females react to the *piropos* also varies according to the region. Women in the highlands are rather shy. They might feel embarrassed and will probably blush. The hotter the climate, the more responsive they are. They might answer back with another *piropo* or with a flood of insults, whichever applies. In the tropics, they may even take the initiative.

Talk about cultural shocks. Just as it took me years to get used to the idea that in Sydney you can walk naked, or dressed in a garbage bag, for all it matters, and men will not look at you – much less say something – I recently found out it can be just as big a shock when it happens the other way.

Case Study: Australian-born female (age 25), second-generation Indu of Portuguese descent – therefore with a Portuguese/Spanish name and olive skin. This particular female spent six months in Cuba in 1997. Being very attractive, she was constantly mistaken for a Cuban *Mulata*, and was subjected to all kinds of *piropos* during her stay. After the first shock, she remembers, she started to answer back, calling men *machistas*. To which they would respond, 'What else do you expect? I am a man.' After a while, she got used to living with *piropos*, and probably even began to enjoy the game.

❧

During your wanderings through the streets and tunnels of Sydney, you made an interesting discovery. This assertion is based on months of solid research and observation; men may not look at anybody in the eyes, but they do look at velvet.

If you are dressed in velvet, never mind that it covers you up to the neck or your skirt is so long it is wiping the floor, men will look at you twice. And not only men, but also women. A most interesting, and probably useful, discovery:

velvet (Macquarie Dictionary): [1] fabric of silk, silk and cotton, or cotton etc, with a thick, soft surface formed of loops with the wraps turned. [2] something likened to the fabric of velvet in softness, etc. [3] the soft, deciduous cov-

ering of a grown antler. [4] a very agreeable or desirable position or situation. [5] money gained through gambling or speculation...

Of course, there's always the appeal of black velvet...

.... when referring to the sexual abuse of female aboriginal servants, Marnie Kennedy cites an aboriginal woman: "we must obey, work hard, do as we are told and be used in any way the white man wishes. White man had a few names he would call us such as 'gins' and 'lubra' and when he wanted a bit of lovin' we were 'black velvet'." [2]

⋄

On reading this very piece, which was originally entitled *The Journey* and is now called *The Tunnel* (and at this moment is still being written, ebbing and flowing like language itself), a friend made an interesting comment – that the velvet image also has a connotation of surface, of superficiality. In your case, a metaphor of how alien it is for you, as a Latina, that many of your relationships with Anglo Saxons are just like velvet: smooth on the surface... but skin deep. [3]

It dawns on you how true this is when you suddenly admit to yourself you have been paying money for meaningful conversations. You have spent a fortune on your hair over the last few years. You have been visiting the

---

2 Huggins, Jackie: 'Firing On in the Mind: Aboriginal Women Domestic Servants in the Inter-War Years', *Hecate* 13, 2, 1987.

3 At the time of writing in 1999, this felt true. Over the following 25 years, the author's connections with Anglo-Australians and fellow Australians of all backgrounds, have profoundly deepened.

hairdresser way more often than necessary, just to get into those deep, inquisitive and very personal conversations he is just so good at...

☙

You get to the train station at the end of the Devonshire Street tunnel, after observing with fascination how many men turn around at the sight of your purple velvet dress. You buy your ticket, get on the train and sit there looking absently out the window, watching the same old houses go past, repeating themselves. Another rolling backdrop. And you think that your life is passing you by just like those houses, while you are glued to your seat without being able to find your voice, to shout that you want the train to stop, that you want to get off.

You realise you often compare your life to a train, a steam train out of control. Trains (and trains going through tunnels) are another of your favourite metaphors.

It is interesting to note that in Greek, the word '*met- aphora*' [metaphor] means transportation, conveyance, transfer, carrying, as well as metaphor. (*Divry's modern English-Greek Dictionary*). Therefore, the word 'train', sig- nifying a means of transport, is literally a metaphor itself...

☙

When you finally arrive at the end of your line, and get off the train – hours, days or perhaps years later – you discover your lover – your Latin lover – is walking beside you, arguing about something irrelevant. And although you haven't been listening, you realise you can hear the echo of your own voice, for you have been arguing back all along.

You wake up in bed to find your lover above you, feeling his weight over your body, his breathing heavy in your ear, the pressure of his lips against your skin. And suddenly you are no longer yourself, but you are him. You can feel what it is like to be inside this woman you love and desire, to feel her cavities, her walls, her tightness. And you go further inside, deeper, penetrating this warm tunnel of crimson velvet, walking through this rainforest of tissue, muscle and arteries, hearing the murmur of the blood stream flowing incessantly, perceiving the movement of the organs... until you feel in the distance the original rhythm, the heartbeat. And delighted, you discover you can hear not one, but two heartbeats, one a lot smaller and faster than the other, unmistakably coming from the womb.

慧

Finally, you reach the end of this body/tunnel, at the head of this woman, who seems to you to be vaguely familiar. You stop for a moment behind the eye sockets, and through her eyes you can see the world, somewhat distorted by her prescription glasses.

There's a fireplace where the fire is crackling, a lamp, a sofa, a dog at her feet and a book on her lap. And you can read what she is reading: the account of someone's surreal journey on trains and through tunnels, and her bizarre thoughts. And you wish if only you could be the writer who would have the imagination to write something like that one day.

This piece of creative non-fiction (or '*verfabula*') was originally published in a longer form in *Waiting in space – an anthology of Australian writing*, edited by Paula Abood, Barry Gamba, and Michelle Kotevski (Pluto Press, 1999). The original version was copyrighted to the editors – published here with permission. Edits have been made.

Tales of Suburban Castaways

Early in the new millennium, several British papers published the story of George Turklebaum, a New York proofreader who had been dead at his desk in an open-plan office for five days before anyone noticed. Turklebaum's employer was quoted in *The Birmingham Sunday Mercury* on 7 January 2001 as saying: 'George was always absorbed in his work and kept much to himself … so no-one found it unusual he was in the same position all that time and didn't say anything.'

If George Turklebaum ever existed, he is probably alive and well; if he is dead, he would be the last to know. The story turned out to be a hoax and has become one of the most popular 'urban legends' of our times. Whoever started the hoax – complete with photographs of both Turkle-baum and his employer, Elliot Wachiaski – managed to fool thousands. Countless emails circulated around the world in several languages, commenting on the endemic indifference of modern society and urging better care of our co-workers and fellow human beings.

The legend of this modern man dead inside a maze of cubicles is reminiscent of the ancient Greek legend of the

Minotaur. With the body of a man and the head of a bull, he inspired so much fear among the inhabitants of Crete that they condemned him to live forever out of sight and out of mind inside a labyrinth.

Argentinian writer Jorge Luis Borges brilliantly reinvented the myth of the Minotaur in his short story *The House of Asterion*. He told the story from the monster's point of view, without revealing his identity until the end. By the time I found out who Asterion really was, I had so identified with him that I was devastated to see him throw himself into the arms of his killer, Theseus. He knew that death was his only way out of the maze where he had been cast away.

Sadly, these two metaphors continue to reflect life around us. Perhaps so many believed the George Turklebaum story because we all know someone who could easily be him. These 'odd' characters, different in some way or another, pop up everywhere, and we tend to avoid them until they become virtually invisible. Whether their differences are physical, psychological, intellectual, cultural or ideological, these suburban castaways are often destined to live behind tangible or intangible walls, ranging from barbed wire to indifference.

Fear and indifference can turn into violence in the blink of an eye. Borges' Asterion was free to walk outside his labyrinth whenever he wanted, but he opted not to, because the only time he did venture out, those who didn't run away in fear, threw stones at him.

Fortunately, human beings also have the capacity to rise above this fear of the 'other', making some castaway stories happier than the tales of George Turklebaum and Asterion. Here is one:

Once, there was a young woman who arrived on these shores with barely a word of English. Coming from a land-locked country, she had never seen the sea before. She was an outsider in a strange land, a female Minotaur lost in the streets of Sydney, a place with a culture as dissimilar to hers as English was to her mother tongue. She didn't understand people's jokes, what 'schoolies' or the Melbourne Cup Sweep were, or what it meant to have a chip on one's shoulder.

For several years, she was the worker who, just like Turklebaum, kept much to herself – in her case, it was due to her limited vocabulary making conversation difficult. But thanks to those who, despite their misgivings, reached out and helped her cross the chasm that separates *them* from *us*, she reached the other side without entirely losing her identity.

This story is not a legend. I was that young woman once.

During my first years in Australia, I desperately tried to blend in, avidly learning the language, reluctantly learning to drink milk in my tea, trying (and failing) to get used to Vegemite on toast in the morning, footy on the weekends and the pub on Friday nights. But no matter how much I tried, I still stood out: I looked different, reasoned differently, spoke with a different accent.

For a while, I found consolation in writing poetry in my mother tongue. To my surprise, my poetry won one prize after another, and my winning poems appeared in the Spanish-language press and were read on SBS radio. In my verses, I explored the metaphors that reflected my new status as an immigrant: grief, death, rebirth, reincarnation, reinvention and the enticing idea of leading a double life. I was 'the typist with the accent' in the office, and the 'published Bolivian poet' in the Spanish-speaking community.

Back in those days, I was living in Western Sydney – a Tower of Babel where people spoke different languages, had a variety of racial backgrounds and seemed alienated inside a melting pot of dreams, hopes, desires and despair. It was not until years later that I read Diane Powell's book *Out West* (Allen & Unwin, 1993). Powell describes Western Sydney as 'a repository for all those social groups and cultures which are outside the prevailing cultural ideal: the poor, the working class, juvenile delinquents, single mothers, welfare recipients, public housing tenants, Aborigines, immigrants.' She introduced me to the idea of *otherness*, a concept that over the years I revisited to exhaustion.

Finally, there was the analogy of translation: I wondered how much of me had been lost in translation. I was *somebody* when I spoke, performed and wrote in Spanish. I was nobody in English.

At the beginning, it was tempting to stay on the periphery, where at least I was somebody amidst fellow outsiders. I even had a small 'fan club' among immigrants who admired the way someone in their early 20s could find the words to express so well their experience of exile. This would be enough for many – but some of us become caught between the tendency to stay within the safety of our labyrinth, and a burning desire to explore the wider world. I wanted to venture out and I did – but, just like Asterion, I made sure one foot always stayed inside.

I lived neither here nor there for many years, trying to

find the courage to face people's fear of my otherness, hoping I would one day stumble upon a magic trampoline that would help me to perform the quantum leap to propel myself out.

Interestingly, the first step in going forwards was to go backwards: I returned to Bolivia for a three-week holiday, and found that I had become even more of a stranger there. My house was no longer my house; my country was no longer my home. My friends and family were still there, but living in what seemed to be a different timeline to which I no longer belonged.

Upon my return, I decided to call the only Anglo-Australian colleague who had been brave enough to invite me for a coffee after work. I had instinctively declined her invitation and had regretted it afterwards. The simple step of making that phone call, felt like a significant win. Over the years I was fortunate enough to find friends, colleagues, employers, mentors and partners who have been willing to take a risk with me. Most of them have even embraced and rejoiced in my differences, making the transition a lot easier.

I have also been back to Bolivia several times since that first visit, and have strengthened my ties and connection to my homeland and its people.

Still, even after breaking the language and acceptance barriers, I will never completely belong in Australia – or anywhere, for that matter. There will always be a certain otherness in me. Then again, there might be a little otherness in every person; a kind of Yin and Yang. In my case, this has become an essential part of my identity. It has followed me outside the labyrinth and sometimes it pulls me back. And old fears occasionally resurface, justified or otherwise.

There was the time when a man in the train heard me talking with my mother in Spanish and reminded us that we live in Australia and should be speaking 'in Australian, like the rest of us'. His attitude hurt us less than the silence of the other passengers – a carriage full of voiceless, faceless people, some of them immigrants like us.

There were those few dark days in December 2005, when racial conflict erupted on the beaches of Sydney and spilled onto the streets and the television sets. We watched people being violently attacked; trains, cars and shops were vandalised and set on fire. For the first time in my 18 years in this country, I was afraid of going out, fearing I could be targeted simply because of my dark eyes, dark hair and foreign looks.

The Australian Government's demonisation of people seeking asylum from war and persecution has also effectively fuelled people's fears of the other. My family arrived in this country by plane, with all our papers in order, but witnessing the treatment of asylum seekers continues to be disheartening.

The email about George Turklebaum started making the rounds again some years after its initial appearance. Even though this time I knew it was a hoax, reading it still brought back memories of the early days when I felt so invisible that I thought it was possible it would take people days to notice if I didn't turn up for work. It also helped me realise, with a shock, that there was a 'George Turklebaum' at that particular workplace and, just like everyone else, I had been ignoring him. When had I become the one who avoided others in the same way I had once been avoided?

True, the crossing of the bridge between 'us' and 'them' hasn't exactly been smooth – it certainly hasn't been as simple as moving from the west to the north of Sydney. Rather than a quantum leap, it is more like a daily balancing act. And yet it continues to be a rewarding and fascinating journey, thanks to the relationships forged, lessons learned and successes achieved along the way. There have been losses, of course. Although I still speak Spanish, I can no longer capture poetic metaphors in that beautiful language, and the talented Bolivian poet is slowly becoming a legend of the past for those who once admired her work.

In the tale of George Turklebaum, it was the cleaner who thought it unusual that the proofreader was still at his desk on a Saturday, reclined over a manuscript. When the cleaner touched him on the shoulder to ask him what was wrong, he discovered the proofreader was stone-cold dead. Indeed, we need not wait until it is too late before we touch our own suburban castaways on the shoulder, to try to help them find their way out of our postmodern labyrinth. Those who are willing to take risks help to create happier endings. It worked for me.

An old Spanish proverb says '*vivir con miedo es vivir a medias*', which translates as 'a life lived in fear is a life half-lived'. The only way to conquer our fear is to defy it – why waste half of the only life we have?

An Exile's Changing Perspectives

My partner John and I are holidaying in Port Stephens, and a waiter asks John, after he places our order, whether we are visiting from England. John was born in England but has been living in Australia for over 30 years. Those with a sensitive ear can pick up his slight cockney accent. John explains he is originally from London and that I am from La Paz, Bolivia.

'From Bolivia!' the young man exclaims. 'Then you must be a very good cook.'

Laughing, we tell him that at home John does most of the cooking. We don't tell him that before I migrated to Australia, I belonged to a professional, upper-middle class family in Bolivia, and that there I never had to cook, do the dishes, clean the floors, or even make my bed. There were indigenous maids to do all that.

Of course, I have learned to do all the household chores since my arrival in Australia at age 19. My mother was unable to sell the family home in Bolivia, as my grandparents were still living in it, and she could not practise her profession of medicine in Australia. Her life savings in bolivianos amounted to less than ten thousand Australian dollars, and thus she became another working-class immigrant who had fled, with her teenage children, a country in political and economic turmoil.

In my experience, apart from assuming that Bolivian women are good cooks, Westerners tend to assume that all Bolivians have the slanted eyes, bronze-coloured skin and high cheeks of the Amerindians. Alas, all I have is the high cheeks, which nevertheless give away my Inca ancestry. Ironically, even in my homeland, Bolivians themselves used to assume I was a foreigner, because of my light skin tone and southern European appearance, and they always treated me with deference.

In Bolivia, John would feel like a film star. Bolivians really look up to *extranjeros* – foreigners – especially if they have fair hair and blue eyes, like him. Caucasians are very rare and they are admired because of their physical appearance, whatever their social status, but for those who were born there, class, name and position are paramount.

Not that I was conscious of the acute class and racial differences or the abject poverty that was all around me while I was growing up in Bolivia. Even after we left the country, my first few years in Australia were crowded by memories that only spoke to me of the colourful homeland and the comfortable life we had lost. What finally opened my eyes was a trip back to the country of my imperfect memories.

All the way on the plane, I remember telling my then husband, Alex, about this mythical land we were going to, where time passed slower that it did in Australia, where there was always an excuse to have a street party, where strangers looked you in the eyes and your neighbours didn't avoid you. Alex couldn't wait to see this place where religion and paganism came together in festivities that were a part of daily life and involved the entire community. This country where indigenous people, with their centuries of culture and tradition, constituted more than half the population.

My narrative was constantly interrupted, as we had to change planes in New Zealand and spend a night in Buenos Aires. Even from Argentina we could not get a direct flight to La Paz, as international airlines refuse to fly their large planes to El Alto International Airport, which sits at over 4000 metres above sea level, surrounded by a treacherous wall of mountains; one of the few airports in the world where planes must ascend before descending.

As the Lloyd Aéreo Boliviano plane, which we boarded in Santa Cruz, approached La Paz, I could already see that the brown, barren landscape didn't match my memories. From the air we could see precarious mud dwellings built at angles that defied gravity on the skirts of the mountains.

In the ensuing weeks I would be in for one shock after another. I didn't remember the narrow streets, the polluted rivers, the absence of trees, the hazardous roads, the chaotic traffic, the dirt and the beggars. Nor did I recall the days when I didn't have the simple things that we take for granted in Australia, such as going to the beach (Bolivia is landlocked), having running hot water, and water that is not only suitable for drinking but is fluoride treated, or walking the street without the fear of being bitten by a rabid dog.

But the greatest shock took place at the family home, the first time we sat to eat lunch with my grandparents. Alex couldn't understand why, when the table in the eat-in kitchen was big enough to sit six, the indigenous maid had to eat in a far corner of the room. She sat on a stool just above the ground, balancing her plate on her knees, discreetly listening to our conversation without saying a word. When Alex asked my grandmother why, she answered matter-of-factly and in front of the maid:

'Because they are not like us; they are a lesser kind of people.'

My grandparents have since passed away, but to this day, the majority of my living relatives would never accept they might have a drop of *sangre de indio* (indigenous blood) in their veins. Personally, I would more readily proclaim my undeniable indigenous ancestry than confess that at the end of the twentieth century, my family and peers still had underpaid indigenous servants in a Third World country.

Back then, in my grandmother's kitchen, the shock wasn't so much provoked by my grandmother's words, but by the realisation of how much my worldview had changed in the five years I had been living in Australia. Grandmother was still the caring, compassionate, God-fearing woman she had always been. She simply believed in the social values she had been indoctrinated in by her ancestors; values that she had instilled in my mother and later passed on to me.

We weren't the only ones who were stunned, though. I remember the look of awe in my grandparents' and the maid's eyes when Alex got up and started washing the dishes after the meal. They had never seen a man do that.

Frankly, I was quite relieved when we left, for I could no longer come to terms with the class differences and the discrimination, the machismo of the society, the corruption and the disorganisation of education and politics. We couldn't help noticing the heavy military presence in the streets, even though the days of the military dictatorship were long gone, and we were almost forced to postpone our date of departure due to a general transport strike.

As the plane descended over Kingsford Smith airport, I saw Sydney from above as if seeing it for the first time, and was overwhelmed by its beauty. The wide roads, the neatness of its layout, the landmarks that stood out from high above, how blue and green it was. I had finally arrived home.

And yet, as a migrant, I must admit the umbilical cord that binds us to our origins cannot be severed during our lifetime.

That trip took place in the early 1990s. A few months after my return to Sydney, I read an article in a women's magazine, which claimed that by the age of 26 (which was my age at the time), the average Bolivian woman would have had at least six children, and would continue to fall pregnant for as long as she slept with her husband. It also claimed that Bolivia had the highest infant mortality rate in South America.

This article astonished me just as much as my three weeks in Bolivia had. In spite of my eye-opening trip, I had not completely grasped the conditions in which the majority of the population lived in the country where I had been born and lived for almost 20 years. I had learned about contraception in the early grades of secondary schooling, and most of my girlfriends in Bolivia only had two children – I had none. It had never occurred to me that the average woman, who belonged to the indigenous class, did not have the basic privileges of health, education and fertility rights that I had enjoyed.

Wanting to make some sort of contribution, I made enquiries about sponsoring a Bolivian child, only to discover that World Vision did not have a program in Bolivia due to its political and economic instability. The documentation came with a profile on the country, which enlightened me to the fact that Bolivia was the second-poorest country in Latin America and one of the poorest in the world.

I have been back to Bolivia a few times since that first trip, for family reasons. During my brief visits, and through the sporadic news I receive from the media, my father and friends who live in Bolivia, I have learned that some things have changed radically in that country over the last few years, while at the same time, very little has changed.

On the health front, UNICEF reports that infant mortality has been halved, from 120 deaths per 1000 births down to 60, thanks to improvements in education and the health system. And yet, it remains one of the highest rates of infant mortality in the western hemisphere. UNICEF also reports that the fertility rate has been dropping steadily, and was down to 3.8 babies per woman in 2004.

On the economic front, a reserve containing some 50 trillion cubic feet of natural gas was discovered in the eastern region of Bolivia in the early 1990s, making this country's reserve one of the largest in the world, according to an article in *Weekly Worker* by Eddie Ford. Alas, Ford also reports that the discovery of this $50-billion bounty has not changed the fact that this is one of the 'most grotesquely unequal societies on earth, as the grinding poverty is disproportionately concentrated amongst those of

Amerindian descent – comprising over 60 per cent of the eight-million population'.

If anything, the discovery of the natural gas reserve has made the country more vulnerable to international predators. The American capitalists, European imperialists, the International Monetary Fund and the World Bank, among others, all want a piece of the pie. The tension between these powers and their desperately poor victims has reached boiling point on more than one occasion in recent years. There was the violent rebellion of 'Black October' in 2003, and the massive demonstrations of May 2005, both of which culminated in dozens of casualties and the ousting of the presidents who failed to stand up to the international corporations that wanted to drain the gas out of the country.

On the socio-political front, there was the unprecedented landslide presidential victory of Evo Morales. He is not only the first indigenous president to be elected in Bolivia's history, but also he has no formal qualifications, comes from a unionist background and is a socialist to boot, much to the horror of the West and the Bolivian middle class. Days after the December 2005 election, several of my mother's relatives and friends in Bolivia contacted my mother asking her about migrating to Australia. They feared a civil war was inevitable; and that they would be killed or kicked out of the country now that the indigenous people were 'taking over' for the first time since Bolivia's first constitution was formulated in 1826.

Morales – or Evo, as everybody calls him – spoke about rewriting the constitution with the input of indigenous leaders, but he did not want the whites to feel threatened.

At his first press-conference Evo declared that 'the poor don't want to be rich; they just want equality'.

My relatives' fears of a civil war between the underprivileged indigenous people and the white/*mestizo* bourgeoisie seem to have been unfounded. At the same time, the hopes and faith the Amerindians put in their new president didn't come to fruition either. In many ways everyone seems to be worse off than before. Even though it is sitting on immense natural wealth, the country is as poor and unstable as ever, with riots, demonstrations, strikes and blockades taking place every day.

In early October 2006, a confrontation between two rival mining groups at the Huanuni mine, one of the world's largest tin mines, led to the indiscriminate throwing of dynamite. The news reported an official death toll of 16, with more than 60 people wounded. Emails from friends in Bolivia reported a much higher number of casualties, some of whom were women and children, though they had not partaken in the fracas. President Evo solved the conflict by dismissing his mining minister, blaming him for not anticipating the violence.

Amidst the chaos, Evo has held onto his post for longer than many of his predecessors have been able to. He continues to defy the US regime in the same way he did as a party leader, when they tried to force the Bolivian government to ban coca farming. One reporter, John Hunt, said that 'it was thanks to his leadership of brave resistance to the US and Bolivian government's coca eradication program that Evo has emerged as the unifying electoral focus for disparate strands of huge popular protest'.

This brings us to the subject of coca-leaf farming, and

inevitably, to cocaine – a drug often mentioned in association with Bolivia in articles and books about this country.

For instance, consider Rusty Young's book *Marching Powder* (2003). This is the 'true' account of Thomas McFadden's experience inside San Pedro prison in La Paz, where he served nearly five years for drug trafficking. The book generated good sales and press coverage in Australia, but sadly it reinforced existing misconceptions that inhabitants on this side of the world might have about an entire country and its people. It was full of statements such as 'hardly anyone in Bolivia admits to taking drugs, but... how could you not take cocaine in a country where a gram is cheaper than a beer?'

Indeed, I seem to contradict all the ideas that Westerners have of Bolivians. My looks are not Amerindian, my cooking skills are minimal, I did not grow up in poverty and I have never consumed cocaine or ever knew, during my 19 years in Bolivia, anyone who consumed cocaine. Then again, I lived in such blissful oblivion for all those years that cocaine snorting might have been happening under my nose, as it were. I do, however, believe that while thousands of indigenous people in Bolivia make their livelihood in the coca-leaf plantations, the majority of them have never seen as much as a gram of the white powder that has made their country infamous.

Admittedly, whilst in Bolivia I have drunk *mate de coca* (coca-leaf tea), which is widely used in the treatment of gastrointestinal complaints, and is excellent for altitude sickness because it stimulates the circulation of blood to the brain. Since time immemorial, coca leaf has been used by Amerindians in a variety of ways: traditional doctors use it as medicine, miners and farmers chew it as a source of strength, and fortune tellers make 'coca-leaf readings'.

Rusty Young's book awoke the archetypal 'Latin temper' in me (in that aspect, I can live up to the expectations). Not happy with saying that all Bolivians are junkies, Young's hero, McFadden, goes on to say they are all stupid, 'because there's not much oxygen up here... Bolivian brains don't develop properly'. I am sure I was not the only reader whose jaw dropped at such declarations.

Paradoxically, *Marching Powder* also gave me an important clue as to why I might have grown up inside a bubble. Reading this book, I remembered something that was seldom mentioned in our household: long before I was born, during the 1950s, my grandfather spent a few months in San Pedro, the same jail from where McFadden narrates his story. Grandfather was not there because of drug trafficking, but because he dared to express a differ-ent political view from the right-wing government of the time. After his short stay at San Pedro, my grandfather, a lawyer, was incarcerated in a concentration camp for two years. He returned a broken man, never able to talk about his experience to the family. He did, however, forbid his children (my mother and her brother) from becoming involved in any type of political activities lest they suffer the same atrocities he was subjected to. Thus, politics was a subject rarely discussed at the home where I grew up.

Perhaps this explains the fact that while attending classical ballet, English and piano lessons, I had no idea babies were dying by the thousands at my doorstep; or that our society was one of the most 'grotesquely unequal' on the planet; or that dictatorships, short lived governments, coups and counter-coups were not commonplace every-where else in the world. It was in Australia, thousands of miles away from my well-meaning, damaged grandfather, that I began to develop an awareness of the socio-economic reality of my country of birth, in the safety of this First World haven where I won't be jailed for my political beliefs.

While enjoying the pleasures of a ferry ride to Nelson Bay – a perfectly blue sky, the endless, magical sea and the sight of dolphins swimming by – I tell John that I continue to marvel at the fortunate life we have here in Australia. Our government is stable, even though we don't necessarily agree with its policies. Our economy is strong, even though we are not happy at the imminence of another interest rate rise. Our surroundings are lush, even though we are in the middle of a drought. Our social system is quite egalitarian, even though people who have not been exposed to the class system of other cultures, might disagree.

In exile, I have become a living contradiction not only to Westerners, but also to Bolivians. My family and childhood friends would be mortified if they knew that in Australia I talk so freely about my indigenous ancestry and they cannot understand why, in my recently developed political awareness, I have decided to identify with the Amerindians. At the same time, they respect me because my partner is a blond, blue-eyed, six-foot tall Englishman. As far as 'going up in the world' goes, I couldn't have done better than that.

This essay was originally published in *Quadrant* magazine, July–August 2007, No 438 (Volume L1, Number 7–8) with the title 'An Exile's View of Bolivia'.

A Bolivian Childhood

Part 1: At the End of the Death Road

One of my first memories is feeling nauseous in the back of a truck, which was precariously descending from the glaciers of La Paz to the tropics of the Yungas on the narrow, winding Death Road in Bolivia. My mother was holding a plastic bag under my chin and I was emptying the contents of my stomach into it, whilst other passengers threw us looks of pity.

At the best of times, I was a scrawny looking child with forlorn eyes, thin limbs and an unusually pale complexion, so I remember our fellow travellers looking genuinely worried. I truly felt I was about to die, but more from embarrassment than from motion sickness.

We were making the trip to visit my father, who was a doctor doing his year of country practice in Irupana, a little town in the Yungas region known mainly for its coffee plantations. We'd boarded a bus in the early hours of the morning, while it was still dark and misty, but as we reached the *cumbre*, the highest and coldest point of the journey, the bus broke down and we were shepherded into the back of a passing truck, our teeth chattering with cold and our breath condensing as it left our mouths.

Back then, I didn't comprehend that I was travelling on one of the most dangerous roads in the world, a two-way dirt road that in some places was no wider than one lane, stretching for 90 kilometres, carved on the side of the mountains at over 4000 metres altitude, with twists and turns so sharp it was often impossible to see any cars coming the opposite way. There were no barriers to stop vehicles from falling over the edge onto cliffs so deep and sheer, that passengers had no chance of surviving. Heavily used, up to 300 people would lose their lives on this road every year and the way was peppered with crosses in memory of those who had perished. Whenever we travelled along this road, and between bouts of nausea, I used to count the crosses as they flew past, thinking that this surely was something that only happened to others.

A few years later, when I was seven years old and my brother two, we came close to becoming one of those crosses when we found ourselves inside my father's car, swaying on the edge of a cliff after he'd miscalculated the angle of a bend and the two wheels on the side ended up off the road. If any of us moved as much as an inch, we would bring about our deaths. We sat tight, afraid to even breathe, refraining from looking at the precipice stretching below us, until other drivers stopped their vehicles to come to our rescue, and pulled the car back on to the road. As though staring death in the face was something that happened to us every day, my father thanked them, got back behind the wheel and we got on with our journey. Nobody spoke about what had just happened.

Years later, when I was in my thirties and living in Australia, a friend emailed me a video compilation of the 'most dangerous roads in the world', in which the Bolivian 'Death Road' featured prominently. I showed it to my mother, and she confessed that when I was aged two, and too young to remember, I had travelled this road at high speed on my father's motorcycle, squeezed between the two of them and wearing no protective gear. Knowing my mother, who is the personification of cautiousness, it was hard to believe she would have agreed to make that motorcycle trip not once, but several times with her infant daughter, but I had to take her word for it.

The following year, when I was old enough to recall the endless bends, the precipices, the landscape morphing in front of our eyes from arid to lavish, and the beautiful 'Bride's Veil' cascade, we made that treacherous trip several times. Until my mother too finished her medical degree and started her own country practice in the same hospital as my father, and we moved to Irupana for that year.

It was the early 1970s and Irupana, like many other regional towns in Bolivia, hadn't yet caught up with the rest of the word. There was no electricity, no television, no telephone. My mother read me books by the light of oil lamps and we listened to battery-operated radios. The hospital was one of the few buildings that had electricity magically produced by a generator. We gorged on strawberries from our neighbour's farm, and drank unpasteurised milk freshly squeezed from their cows, with a deliciously thick layer of cream. At night, we plucked oranges from the trees in our backyard and my father roasted them in a bonfire.

The first movie I saw was projected on a white sheet hung on the wall of an improvised theatre in town, where we sat on folding chairs scattered on the dirt. The movie was Walt Disney's *Pinocchio* and I enjoyed it immensely – until Pinocchio got swallowed by the whale. This seemed completely unfair and I cried, kicked and screamed as though it was the end of the world, and we had to abandon the screening to pacify the other moviegoers; it was not often they got to see moving pictures.

The edges of my first memories are soft and dreamlike. They started in this tiny, backward town where every-thing seemed to take place in slow motion. Irupana was surrounded by rolling green hills, plantations and tropi-cal valleys. At only a few hours' distance from the barren, high-altitude, noisy La Paz city, this was a completely dif-ferent world.

After being attacked by two different dogs – though one of the bites, from our own dog, was completely my fault – while under the watch of two different babysitters, my parents gave up on the idea of having me looked after by nannies and decided to send me to school.

The nearest school was an all-boys school. Neither my gender nor my age (I was three years and a few months old) deterred the headmaster, and I was allowed to join the kindergarten class. Not only was I the only girl at the school, but I was the youngest by almost two years. I was also the palest, as most of the inhabitants of Irupana had the copper skin tone of the Amerindians. Although there were some European immigrants in this area, most of the population was indigenous. Even in the city, my skin was unusually white in comparison to most Bolivians as a result of having some French and English blood somewhere down the line. At kindy I was not teased because of my differences – quite the contrary, I was the centre of everyone's attention, from the teachers to the kids, and I basked in it.

We presented a theatrical version of *Snow White and the Seven Dwarfs* at the end of the year, and I was given the title role – it would have been quite upsetting if I hadn't got the part, being the only girl in the troupe; even the witch was played by a boy. My grandmother helped my mother make a pink maxi dress for the performance and newspapers were carefully laid on the dusty stage floor to avoid ruining my outfit when I fell to the ground, after taking a bite of the enchanted apple.

Despite the dog incidents, this was a magical year, but 12 months flew by and we had to return to the big city at the other end of the Death Road.

п

Part 2: Growing up in Miraflores

After spending 12 months in the rustic town of Irupana, we returned to the hustle and bustle of La Paz city, with its congested, labyrinthine streets, filled with dilapidated buildings, antiquated cars, overloaded buses, street vendors, food stalls, beggars, stray dogs and the ever-present noise of car horns.

To this day, there is always some kind of trouble in La Paz; strikes, blockades and demonstrations are a daily occurrence. In the early 1970s, however, we were at the start of a more or less stable period in political history, under the dictatorship of General Hugo Banzer Suárez.

Of course, at this time I was oblivious to all of this. I was four years old and all I knew was that we lived in a neighbourhood called Miraflores, far enough from the centre of the city to be relatively quiet, and close enough for us to drive there within 15 minutes, though usually it took much longer due to the horrendous traffic.

Our cobbled street was one block long and at the end of it there was a muddy, slippery path that led to the bed of a polluted river. Unfortunately, some people in the street had decided that this 'no man's land' was a good place to dispose of their rubbish. We had a garbage collection truck that came once a week. A bell announced its arrival and the maids ran outside with their bins to catch it, but those who missed it threw their rubbish down the road, much to the delight of the stray dogs and to the despair of the residents.

At the top of the street there was a small park, with the statue of Baden Powell, known to all of us as the Scout Park. There were three corner shops in the streets surrounding the park and an ever-popular handball field. Two blocks from our place were the beautiful botanical gardens.

Shortly after we returned from Irupana, both my parents obtained scholarships to do their master's degrees, in the Middle East of all places. They set off for a year, leaving me in the care of my grandparents. My grandparents owned a three-storey building consisting of three apartments. They lived on the top floor and the other two apartments were rented out. My parents' home was at the back, separated by a courtyard, so I didn't have to move very far.

Instructed by my mother, Grandma enrolled me at the local school. Even though I was still too young, the headmaster, just like the one in Irupana, gave no objection. When he allowed me to start at the school two years ahead of time, his reasoning was that I could repeat the grade at the end of the year. Instead, I passed with flying colours. For three consecutive years, I represented my class as 'Princess of Study' at the spring pageant due to my good marks. As a result, I would be two years ahead of my classmates for the rest of my school life, and many years later would find myself at university at 16, feeling quite out of place in a psychology course that many mature students were doing as their second degree.

At age four, however, I was quite happy to be the smallest child in the whole school. Grandma walked me to school every day. She was a formidable woman in her early fifties, who looked much younger than her age. I was her first and only grandchild at this stage and she was delighted to take on the role of both mother and father for a year, though the task was easier because, like most middle-class ladies in Bolivia, she had a live-in maid to help.

It was hard to know what Grandpa thought about my parents' absence, or the fact that a four-year-old child who never shut up had moved into his home for a year, or anything else. A busy lawyer, he made himself scarce; when he was not in his office or in court, he spent his time in his study or in the enormous basement beneath the house, where he had room after room filled with carpentry equipment. He was a carpenter at heart, though the results of his labour were always somewhat wobbly.

Because I was so small, my teacher, Miss Teresa, didn't

think it was safe for me to be out in the playground during recess, lest I got trampled on by the other students. She ushered me with her into the kiosk, where she moonlighted as a candy and refreshments seller. Thus, I spent my breaks sitting on a stool in the kiosk while Miss Teresa (who was not a Miss at all; she had several children and grandchildren) fended off the crowds of hungry students.

Halfway through the year my parents returned from overseas. The degree was taught in English and my father couldn't pick up the language in the short time they had to learn it. He had grown his beard and in the photos they brought back, he looked just like a local. They were deeply disappointed about not finishing their master's this time around, though I suspected my grandparents were relieved; in 1972, with the Israel–Palestine conflict in full swing, the Middle East was not the best place to be spending a year.

I always had terrible teeth, and my baby teeth had to be extracted months before the permanent set was due to come out. I wasn't happy about having to wear false teeth, but made the best of it. When I was finally a little bigger and allowed to play outside the kiosk, I would take my false teeth out, turn them over so that the pointy red corners that were meant to go in the palate stuck out like bloody fangs, and spend my recesses chasing my classmates as they playfully fled screaming 'vampire!'

My birthdays were always celebrated with a well-attended party, with plenty of presents and homemade treats, a big cake, and the traditional cardboard piñata full of sweets and small toys. As the birthday girl, I got to bash the poor piñata with a stick while blindfolded, so that the other kids could fight over the contents when it finally burst open after several misses. And fight they did, with much shouting, wrestling and hair-pulling taking place on the ground.

My brother arrived when I was five and a half years old. He was born on 28 December, the 'Day of the Holy Innocents' in the biblical calendar, which is the equivalent of April Fools' Day – when people play pranks on each other. That morning, I was woken by an uncle, who told me that everyone was at the hospital because my brother was born that morning. The baby was not due to arrive for some time, so my first reaction was to laugh, thinking my uncle was playing an 'innocents' joke on me. Then I realised he was serious, and that my baby brother, with whom I would soon be sharing a bedroom and my family's affections, was on his way home. And just like that, my reign as a sole child and grandchild was over.

In Transit

I am sitting in the Transit Lounge at a poorly lit, almost deserted airport. In the distance I hear the sound of an industrial vacuum cleaner, and every now and then a security guard does his rounds and checks on me. Apart from that, there seems to be no-one else in this place.

It's sometime after midnight and my flight to Buenos Aires doesn't depart till three am. Once there, I have to wait eight hours for the connecting flight that will take me to Sydney via New Zealand. I am not looking forward to the tedious wait at another airport, or the 16 hours flying time that will follow. I admire those who can do long-haul travelling on a regular basis. I can hardly manage it once every few years. The last time I made this trip was to bury my paternal grandmother, and this time it was to attend my maternal grandmother's funeral.

My mother has been doing this trip every second year, to visit her parents. She tried various routes; via Los Angeles, via Santiago de Chile[4]; via Buenos Aires.

---

4 In 2024, we read that the flight route Santiago de Chile–Santa Cruz, which we took several times, was officially the most turbulent route in the world, ranked via eddy dissipation rate (EDR).

They were all equally long and complicated, involving at least four flights.

Mum won't be making this trip very often now that both her parents have passed away. Grandad died in January; Grandma followed less than three months later. Bolivians bury their dead the very next day, so they had to embalm Grandma's body in order to allow for the three days it would take us to arrive.

I'm returning to Sydney on my own because Mum had to stay to clean up her parents' house and dispose of the contents. She has to find homes for all the furniture, clothes, pictures, hundreds of books, a piano, antique mirrors, the sewing and knitting machines, the white goods, the carpentry workshop in the basement. Not to mention all the 'special occasion' silverware, crystals and porcelain crockery, some of it still in the original packaging it came in when it was gifted to my grandparents on their wedding day.

All that's going back to Australia with me are a few tablecloths, a rosary, a handful of photographs, and a little plastic angel Grandma had on her bedside table at the time of her death.

❧

When they buried Grandma, they had to open the family grave. Before they lowered her coffin, we noticed that Grandpa's casket was ruptured at both ends; we could see his shoes and a few strands of his thick hair. Apparently as the bodies decompose, they swell up and release gases; the combination of these two things can make the wood explode.

'But that won't happen to your Grandma,' Mum explained after the funeral, 'because she was embalmed. She will remain unchanged forever.'

'They did that to Eva Peron,' said an uncle. 'When she died, they embalmed her body; but they didn't bury it. They kept it in the house and they would change her clothes, do her hair, sit her at the lounge or at the table sometimes, like a life-size doll, until her husband died. Only then, they buried them together.'

We didn't know whether this was macabre or amusing. We decided it was amusing.

'We could have done the same with Grandma,' I said. 'We could have dressed her up in her Sunday best, and taken her on the plane to Australia with us.'

Grandma had been partially blind for almost 20 years and this deterred her from leaving the house, let alone undertaking the three-day journey to Australia. She never came to visit us.

'Now that she's a free spirit, she's probably already there, waiting for us,' Mum said.

'No,' the uncle corrected her. 'Don't forget that her spirit remains here, in the house, until after the eight-day mass. She's still in transit between here and the afterlife.'

೮೩

Suddenly it's not so lonely here at the airport. I feel that Grandma's spirit, no longer in transit, is with me while I wait at this empty passenger lounge. She's accompanying me in this long trip and she's also accompanying Mum through the difficult task of sorting out her possessions and all the memories attached to them. As I drift in and out of consciousness, I am no longer afraid to fall asleep and miss my plane; she will wake me up when it's time to board.

I hate the waiting, I hate planes, I hate air-sickness. But I don't regret having made the trip, even if it was only for a couple of weeks. I only regret one thing: I didn't get to speak with Grandma before she died.

໕

After my grandfather's death, Grandma found herself practically alone in their huge house. My first cousin, also her granddaughter, was keeping her company – but the rest of her family had moved interstate. Grandma didn't want to leave her house at any cost, and when faced with a future alone, wandering blind from room to room, she decided to die.

One day in mid-April, she gave my cousin the money needed to pay for her funeral plus US$1000, which was a small fortune in Bolivia, that she had set aside to cover the family grave with slabs of marble. She had always lived a frugal lifestyle, but for some reason she wanted her grave to stand out from the rest. Then, she took to bed. Shortly afterwards, my cousin had to go interstate to stay with her family, so they employed a 19-year-old, Marisol, to keep Grandma company and help around the house.

Grandma didn't have a terminal illness, and although she was fragile and had been coughing for a few months, she was certainly not dying. At least that's what relatives and friends reported. Meanwhile Mum, all the way in Sydney, was trying to decide whether she should make arrangements to travel immediately or not, since Grandma was not actually unwell. At 82 and partly blind, Grandma was still fiercely independent.

Finally, Mum made up her mind to go and I decided to fly with her. We booked our tickets to fly out on Anzac Day. Grandma died of 'natural causes' two days before our flight.

℞

Marisol, the young woman who was hired to look after Grandma in the last weeks of her life, told us two stories.

First, she said Grandma was so scared of dying alone in her sleep that she asked Marisol to sleep next to her. Marisol was woken one night by Grandma talking in her dreams. Her speech was very clear, and Marisol discerned that she was speaking with Grandpa.

'Don't be in such a rush, old man,' she was saying. 'I'm only waiting for them. They'll be here soon.' She knew we had decided to come as soon as we realised that she might have been serious about her impending death. But Grandpa, who had been an impatient man in life, couldn't wait even after he had passed.

The second story concerns a dream Marisol had the night after Grandma died. The wakes in Bolivia are held *before* the funeral – that is the point of them: in case the deceased 'wakes up' because they are not actually dead. As the wake was going to be hosted at the family home, the coffin remained in the living room for three days, waiting for us to arrive. During that time, Marisol slept alone in the house, keeping Grandma company.

Marisol dreamed that Grandma was calling to her from

inside the coffin, knocking on the see-through window.

'Marisol! Get me out of here,' she was saying. 'What am I doing here, anyway? I'm supposed to wait for my daughter in my own bed. Take me to the bed now.' So Marisol, in her dream, took Grandma out of the coffin and helped her to the bed. 'She was very stiff, like a zombie,' Marisol said.

When Dad heard that story at the wake, he said he would demand to be buried with his mobile phone. He attended the wake with his second wife, and his brothers and sisters were also there, though some were remaining in separate rooms due to a family feud.

␣

While Grandma was still 'in transit' and her spirit was, according to belief, floating around the house the week after her death, Mum and I slept in her room. Even though there were three bedrooms in the huge apartment, we shared my grandparents' double bed, keeping each other company. Mum told me family anecdotes that Grandma had shared with her, and I entertained her with the latest upheavals of my love life.

Often, when we were talking about Grandma or about something that concerned her, the lamp on her bedside table would light up, sometimes with a soft flash, sometimes a brighter one. While I was trying not to freak out at this, Mum was quite thrilled to be able to communicate with Grandma. A soft flash meant no, a bright one yes.

After a few days the phenomenon stopped and we forgot all about it. But one morning, whilst we were going through Grandma's wardrobe, I asked Mum what she was planning to do with Grandma's jewellery.

'She didn't have a lot of jewellery,' Mum said. 'And she gave most of it away already. She gave me a few items last year and... didn't she give you some when you came here last?'

Five years earlier, Grandma had indeed given me two beautiful rings, a pair of earrings, a gold pendant, and a watch. Unfortunately, shortly after I went back to Sydney, my apartment was broken into. The rings, which were on top of my dresser, were stolen along with other valuables. The other items survived because they were hidden away. I had asked Mum not to tell Grandma because that was part of my inheritance and I didn't want to upset her. With the insurance money I purchased similar rings, but they would never be the same.

'That's right.' Mum remembered that day in my grandparents' bedroom. 'Grandma gave you her rings, and she died without ever knowing they were stolen.'

FLASH... the lamp lit up – brightly this time.

Mum and I looked at each other with consternation.

'Uh-oh...' We said in unison. 'She knows now.'

ೞ

A few days later, on 5 May – Grandpa's birthday – I managed to get their old record player to work. Mum and I played a few 45s, ancient and scratched, and we danced.

Mum looked at the empty living and dining rooms – the furniture had been taken away already – and sighed.

'I had a few good parties in this place, in the 1950s and 1960s,' she said. 'Your grandma and your uncle would take turns at the piano while we danced the night away.'

'And I had the best parties here in the 1980s,' I said. When I was at university, my grandparents' house was the designated venue for all our gatherings.

We toasted with lemon tea to the happy memories lived by the three generations who had gone through that house.

⚃

It's nearly two am; the check-in desks are now open and people are arriving to board the flight to Buenos Aires. I gather my luggage and my thoughts, both the happy and the melancholy ones, and make a move. In about 37 hours I will be back home in Sydney.

I started to call Sydney home after my first visit back to Bolivia, but there was always my grandparents' home, the home where I grew up, where I'd lived some of the best years of my life, anchoring part of my soul back there. Thus, I myself have been 'in transit', in between two countries and two homes, for more than 14 years.

Grandma, I am sorry I am not there to bring flowers to your marble grave; I am thousands of kilometres away. But I've decided, as you would have liked, to rejoice rather than weep.

I am glad you have completed your voyage from this life into the next. I am glad Mum can now get on with her own life instead of being torn between her children who have settled in Australia, and her parents who didn't want to leave their country. As for me, in a strange way I am glad I no longer have a 'home' to go back to in Bolivia, for this means I can finally call Australia my only home.

Although Grandma just whispered in my ear she has the suspicion that, along with my mother, my brother and millions of others who leave their homelands, by choice or otherwise, I am destined to live 'in transit' until we meet again in the afterlife.

Use Your Power to Inspire

Do you remember the person who inspired you the most?

I am not referring to a role model, famous author, or historical figure. Think of the teacher, parent, mentor or friend who recognised a particular talent you possess and who, by encouraging you to pursue it, helped define the person you went on to become.

She or he might have been an influential figure in your formative years, or they might have made their appearance later in life. This is what happened in Mem's case.

Mem was a mature-age student in her early thirties when she decided to take a course in children's literature at Flinders University in South Australia, mainly because she wanted to learn about books that would interest her inquisitive seven-year-old daughter. The year was 1978.

Shortly after starting the course, Mem was surprised to discover that one of her assignments entailed writing a children's book. Not because the task was too difficult, but because she thought it would be too easy – not the type of assignment she was expecting to do in this highly demanding, academic course.

This assignment proved to be one of the hardest she ever completed, and through the process she developed new respect for children's authors. The result was a four-and-a-half-page story she called *Hush, the Invisible Mouse*.

She never intended to do anything with this assignment after submitting it, apart from perhaps reading it to her daughter. Her lecturer, however, was so impressed by it that she urged her to try to have it published. Her lecturer showed such faith in the story that Mem decided to follow her advice. Little did she know this would be the start of a five-year odyssey during which she sent the story, accompanied by illustrations done by her friend Julie, to publisher after publisher, receiving rejection after rejection.

The tenth publisher accepted it, but asked her to make major changes, including cutting the story by two thirds, rewriting what was left of it in a more lyrical style, and changing the mice to another species altogether. Finally in 1983, Mem Fox published her book with the new title *Possum Magic*, illustrated by Julie Vivas.

Possum Magic has gone on to sell over five million copies, becoming and remaining the most popular and best-selling picture book in Australia. To this day, Mem Fox acknowledges Felicity Hughes, the teacher who encouraged her, whenever she talks about the amazing 'story behind the story' of *Possum Magic*.

Sometimes, all it takes is one person to believe in you.

In my life, I have received encouragement and inspiration from a great many people – educators, family, friends, employers, and even people I hardly know. But one of my earliest memories of profound influence is that of my fourth-grade teacher, Miss Sarah.

I was eight years old and still living in La Paz, Bolivia. One day, instead of the customary apple, I gave Miss Sarah a poem entitled 'To My Teacher'. I never expected her to carry on about it as much as she did. She was so thrilled with it, she insisted I perform it at Teacher's Day assembly.

I memorised my poem but half way through, I forgot my own verses and ran off the stage in tears, in front of an audience of hundreds.

This might not have been a very auspicious start to a career in public performance, but Miss Sarah's encouragement imbued in me what would become a lifetime love for poetry, and inspired me to keep on writing. I never went on to sell millions of copies of my poems (let's face it – how many people do?) but we all know that sales and figures are not, or should not be, a measure of success.

It was the belief of people like Miss Sarah that also inspired me to write creatively in English, when I moved to Australia. After I had been in this country for several years, I gathered the courage, with the encouragement of mentors and friends, to submit one of my essays to a mainstream literary magazine, *Quadrant*. Until then, I had published my work only in Spanish, or in English but in 'multicultural' anthologies.

Lauded Australian poet Les Murray, who has since passed away, was the literary editor at the time. As part of his feedback, he said: 'Your English is impeccable and obviously adequate for literary writing in your new(er) language'. Admittedly, he wrote this as a prelude to rejecting the piece, but I will treasure this note not only because it was handwritten by Les Murray himself, but also because only a few years before, when I was still struggling to grasp the use of everyday English, I often despaired that I would ever be able to write at a literary level in my second language.

But Mr Murray didn't completely reject my piece. He highlighted one aspect that he was interested in, and invited me to develop that into something longer. The result was my essay 'An Exile's View of Bolivia', which was eventually published in *Quadrant* and is also included in this collection with a different title. It was the beginning of a fruitful and rewarding journey writing in my new(er) voice.

Think of how rewarding it would be if you were the person who changed someone's life, by noticing and encouraging a talent that might not be so evident to others, not even to themselves. Felicity Hughes saw that gift in a four-page story about a mouse. You don't need to be an expert in any field to be able to recognise when someone has a particular talent, big or small. If there is a person – young or mature – who you think is good at something, make sure you point it out.

Even if it is a talent for writing poetry; it will rarely bring them fame or fortune, but it is likely to bring them happiness. As Franklin D. Roosevelt said, 'Happiness lies in the joy of achievement and the thrill of creative effort.'

Although in some cases, writing great poetry can lead to great things: Mr Less Murray received the Australian Literature Society's Gold Medal and the Queen's Gold Medal for Poetry, and his work has been translated into at least 10 languages.

My thanks to Mem Fox for agreeing (through her literary agent, Jenny Darling) to the retelling of the 'story behind the story' of *Possum Magic*.

Words versus Pictures

They say 'a picture tells a thousand words', but much as I like taking, printing (yes, I still print my favourite snaps) and sharing pictures, I much prefer to tell a story using words.

Some years ago, a friend invited me to her grandson's christening. As a child in Bolivia, I was raised a Catholic, but it had been a long time since I'd attended mass. I found the sermon refreshing, although not necessarily from a faith perspective. The priest started by showing the infamous 'selfie' that President Barack Obama, British Prime Minister David Cameron and Denmark's Prime Minister Helle Thorning Schmidt took of themselves at Nelson Mandela's memorial service. Even on that solemn occasion, they couldn't help themselves and succumbed to the temptation of taking a selfie. And they were caught in the act, by another camera.

The priest then showed a 'selfie' he took of himself at the Wailing Wall in Jerusalem. He said that the 'selfie' is our modern way of showing the world 'I was there' with that famous person, or at that famous place, and I have the photo to prove it. It is our way of 'witnessing' events, landmarks, encounters and, more often than not, trivial moments in our lives.

Before the invention of cameras, and more recently, digital cameras and smartphones, people documented their encounters, travels and experiences by writing them down. The priest referred to the gospels, particularly the gospels written by John and Matthew, who were two of the 12 apostles, and as such witnessed first hand the life and deeds of Jesus, the most famous and enduring 'celebrity' of all. The gospel writers couldn't take 'selfies' of themselves with Christ, so they wrote everything they saw to document it, and their stories spread like lightning – or in modern terms, they went 'viral'.

Nowadays, with everybody carrying a camera in their pocket, selfies, photographs and videos documenting our lives minute by minute are overloading the media landscape. Social media posts that don't include a picture or video don't receive as many 'likes'. Images and reels are much more likely to be shared than plain text. Media releases with photographs have a much higher chance of being published. We live in a visual era, and words without pictures are often overlooked. People take thousands of photographs of every trip or special occasion, but how often do they look at, or even download those pictures?

When I travelled to Europe in the pre-digital age, I took a grand total of 144 photographs: six rolls of 24. Nowadays, that is a laughable quantity for a three-week tour, but when I returned home and developed the rolls, I could hardly remember what photo was taken where. Fortunately, I had taken a comprehensive travel diary as well, describing the places, their history, the people I met at every stop, and other interesting facts. I was able to marry the words with the pictures, and the resulting illustrated story, which I printed out and shared with friends, was much more effective in conveying my adventures than the photo albums I produce these days, which have a one-line caption per photo and sometimes not even that.

A few months ago, I was driving home after work and I witnessed an incredible rainbow. At first I felt frustrated because I couldn't stop to take a photo, but then I realised that sometimes we miss the moment by trying to capture it with a camera. I captured it with my eyes, committed it to my memory, and that was enough.

I still remember the highlight of my first trip to Adelaide, South Australia. In my diary, I recorded Womadelaide (the music festival at the botanical gardens) as one of the highlights; also day trips to Hahndorf and Victor Harbor, and a cruise down the Murray River.

But the most priceless highlight of that trip was the sunset over West Beach on the Tuesday night when we arrived. It had been a hot afternoon so we walked to the beach to cool down. While we were there, the cloudy sky turned into an incredible canvas with colours, textures and shapes in constant motion. The sea became a liquid mirror of the sky, reflecting the silver, blue and pink hues of the clouds, and the effect of the sun setting over the water was stunning. This was particularly awe-inspiring to me, because I had never seen the sun set over the sea.

People quickly began to arrive, sensing something momentous was taking place; some of them were even carrying champagne and glasses. We all stood there, clinking glasses and taking in the landscape with jaws dropped.

I cursed myself for not having my camera with me, but then again, a photo would have never paid that moment justice. Instead, I wrote it all down as soon as we returned to our hotel. We went back to the beach at the same time the next day, with some friends who'd arrived that morning, but unfortunately for them the sunset was nothing more than ordinary.

Decades later, I don't remember much about the Hahndorf and Victor Harbor excursions or the cruise on the Murray, even though I took copious pictures of those places. But when I read my travel diary, I can instantly recall 'that' sunset, which remains in my mind as one of the most spectacular I have ever seen.

To be able to conjure a visual image after all these years by painting it with words, demonstrates – to me – the supremacy of words over pictures. It might take an hour to write one thousand words (as it did to write this 988-word piece), and less than a second to take a picture, but it is time well spent.

From the Indian to the Pacific — an Epic Train Journey

When I first heard about the legendary *Indian Pacific* train journey, the expression 'bucket list' hadn't been invented yet. It was the late 1980s and I was newly arrived in Australia.

I have always been fascinated by trains, and had used them a handful of times in Bolivia to travel between cities. My fascination reached new heights when I moved to Sydney, a city so large that people used trains to commute between suburbs! Furthermore, there were these amazing printed leaflets called 'timetables', which helped commuters plan their journey with a great degree of accuracy. Timetables, as far as public transport was concerned, were an alien concept to us until we moved to Australia. If buses in Bolivia run to timetables, these are never revealed to customers.

From the moment I heard about it, the notion of spending three days and three nights aboard a sleeper car, traversing the entire Australian continent from west to east, from the Indian Ocean to the Pacific, while seeing the entire breadth of this vast country, acquired the quality of a dream. A dream that lodged itself inside my mind along with the other adventures I hope to have 'one day before I die'.

The year my mother and I celebrated 25 years of living in Australia, we wanted to do something special to mark the occasion. It surfaced that this archetypal Australian journey was also on her 'bucket list'. So, bookings were made for July, and we boarded the *Indian Pacific* at East Perth station on the day before my birthday, carrying expectations as heavy as our luggage. My suitcase was particularly heavy with the weight of board games, books and crossword puzzles, taken in case we became bored.

☙

The Journey

The *Indian Pacific*'s journey spans 4,350 kilometres. At an average of 85 kilometres per hour, it takes 65 hours from go to whoa. Our train, which had 25 carriages, was nearly 600 metres long, including the locomotive. The dining car, Queen Adelaide Restaurant, was six cars away. Getting to the restaurant was a journey in itself, through narrow corridors, opening and closing doors, creaky passageways, and endless rows of windows and cabins. Manoeuvring around other passengers walking the opposite way was a feat, particularly those who were elderly and frail – of which there were many.

Our cabin was 'cosy', but we didn't feel cramped. While we had our dinner, a 'magic fairy' came to our cabin and readied our bunk beds for sleeping, and also came back in the morning, while we enjoyed a leisurely breakfast, to convert our beds back into comfortable seats, clean the ensuite and change the towels.

Even breakfast was a three-course affair: tea, coffee or juice as starters, cereal or fruit compote as entrée; and blueberry pancakes, bagels with jam and fresh cream, or a full cooked breakfast for main. The superb lunch and dinner menus included seafood, chicken, kangaroo, fish, steak, soup and vegetarian meals to choose from, not to mention desserts such as panna cotta with lavender-flavoured fairy floss, all washed down with as many drinks as desired, and all included in the fare. My glucose readings remained sky high throughout the trip. I didn't advise them of any special dietary requirements – if eating so well meant that this diabetic would be cutting three days at the end of her life, so be it. Feeling adventurous, I even tried kangaroo filet mignon.

Our cabin faced west, which meant we were travelling backwards. I was slightly put off by this, but even in this regard it didn't disappoint. When we arrived in Adelaide, and whilst we were exploring the city sights, the locomotive was switched from the front to the back, so that those passengers who were travelling backwards would face the front for the remainder of the journey. Still, facing west had its advantages: I was able to appreciate the deep orange-purple hues of the sunset on the first night.

Our off-train excursion to Kalgoorlie, 'Queen of the Golden Mile', in Western Australia, started at nearly 11 pm. Being so late, we expected a quick tour of the main streets and a brief stop at the 'super pit', the massive gold mine at the heart of the town, which operates 24 hours a day.

Instead, it took almost two hours, including a visit to a museum, refreshments, and two demonstrative talks. I welcomed the first moments of my birthday on top of a giant dump truck whose wheels were twice as tall as me. By the time we returned to our cabin at 1.10 am, after driving through the infamous Hay Street, where only two brothels remained, we were wide awake. We spent a restless night hearing the humming and rattling of the train, and the screeching noises it made, which reminded me of whale songs, as it turned corners.

We spent most of my birthday crossing the Nullarbor plain – from the Latin words 'null' and 'arbor', meaning 'no trees'. Despite the name, nearly 800 species of plant grow in that region, and there is no shortage of wildlife either – camels, wedge-tailed eagles, lizards, snakes, wombats, red kangaroos, dingoes and emus, although we didn't see any of these animals at all. That section of the track is the longest stretch of railway line running in a straight line in the world: 485 kilometres. From our window, the desert was so vast I thought I could see the curvature of the earth.

We had the chance to stretch our legs in the ghost town of Cook. The town was officially closed in 1997, although diesel locomotives, including the *Indian Pacific*, continue to stop there for refuelling. Due to this, it still had a population of '4 people, 2 cats, 20 chooks, 30 dingoes ... and 2 million flies'.

We slept better the second night and got up at 6.00 am the next day to have a quick breakfast before boarding a bus for our 'city highlights' tour of Adelaide, South Australia. We left Adelaide facing forwards, sliding through fertile fields, flat and green, stretching as far as the eye could see

– a startling contrast to the landscape of the previous day. By the afternoon, we had entered the Outback: red earth, grey bushes and gum trees, with the sun hanging low on a sky scattered with clouds.

The last off-train excursion was at Broken Hill, New South Wales, where we were greeted by a spectacular sunset. We were shown the town's main streets, all named after minerals: Sulphide, Bromide, Argent… and learned about the history of this once burgeoning gold town. The tour concluded with drinks at the Palace Hotel, which began in 1889 as a coffee palace. It became famous in the 1990s after the movie *Priscilla, Queen of the Desert* was partly filmed there. We were welcomed in true Priscilla style by a 68-year-old drag queen, who showed us the artistic murals painted on the walls and ceilings by Mario Celetto and Indigenous artist Gordon Waye.

After another delicious dinner aboard the train, we slept through another night and woke up to the sight of a magnificent rainbow arching over the Megalong Valley in the Blue Mountains. Soon we were speeding through the outskirts of Sydney, crossing the Nepean River, and arriving at Central station, where our adventure came to an end. On my first night back at home, I was sure my bed was rocking and swaying through the night.

❧

Reflections

For me, this journey was an opportunity to pause and reflect, to enjoy a few days without having to think about schedules and deadlines, fulfilling commitments, or rushing somewhere as I always seem to be doing. A chance to sit and relax without staring at a computer or mobile phone screen, back to the basics of pen and paper, an old-fashioned book, some relaxing music, the *Indian Pacific* 'bush' radio channel, and the living, breathing landscape of my incredible adopted country as the main entertainment, which at times was relaxing and at other times hypnotic.

I read one whole book in a day, and wrote prolifically in my travel diary. My mother brought her book and her knitting, but didn't progress much with either – often I found her snoozing without guilt, stretched across the seat, lulled by the rhythm of the train. We didn't even unpack the crosswords or board games that I'd carted all the way. In any case, there were plenty of games and willing, friendly adversaries in the Outback Explorer Lounge, which was always buzzing with the chatter of people and the clinking of glasses.

Most of the people aboard the *Indian Pacific* were retirees. At the time, retirement was still a couple of decades away for me, a future so far away it seemed to belong to another country. I was thankful to have been able to tick this bucket-list item while I still had the funds, stamina and a pair of strong legs, even if that meant that I was accompanied by people who were significantly older than me. If anything, it made me feel very young; and when we saw the way in which some passengers were struggling to walk around the moving carriages or to get on and off the train (particularly the gentleman in a wheelchair with an oxygen bottle attached), even my sixty-seven-year-old mother said she felt like a spring chicken.

Two years later, Mum and I had the opportunity to cross the 2,979 kilometres that separate Darwin from Adelaide, aboard *The Ghan*. Travelling on *The Ghan* is traditionally a three-day, two-night journey, but we were fortunate to be among the first to do '*The Ghan* Expedition', which included an extra day with an overnight stay in Alice Springs. Highlights comprised a visit to the majestic Nitmiluk Gorge in Katherine, a tour of Alice Springs, lunch at the Alice Springs Telegraph Station, an Aussie Barbeque Dinner under the stars, and half a day in Coober Pedy, the 'Opal Capital of the World'. On the last day, we watched the sunset while sipping champagne at the Breakaways, a desert-like landscape with beautiful, red-coloured rock formations; and returned to *The Ghan* on time for dinner around a bonfire.

Both journeys were extravagantly expensive for people on our income, but they were worth every cent. We both grew up in a landlocked country – Bolivia was not always landlocked, but that is another story – and in my case, I never saw the ocean until the age of 20. So, even though I have travelled extensively here and abroad, few experiences compare to traversing an entire continent, from ocean to ocean, west to east and north to south, on a sleeper train.

The Perfect Christmas Gift

It is not often I burst into tears when receiving a gift, but this is what happened one Christmas morning when I opened a present from my partner, John.

First, he explained that it had been a small odyssey finding this gift. He had been looking for it for years, and had found and ordered it from two online catalogues in Australia. But in both cases his orders were cancelled because they didn't have the item in stock. Finally, he bought it from an online merchant in the United States, who sent it by express post to ensure its arrival before Christmas – it arrived on Christmas Eve. After all that effort, John hoped I would like it, but he didn't expect me to cry. He knew, at that moment, that his efforts had been worth it.

The parcel had the shape, feel and weight of a thick hardcover book. The first thing I saw was the author's name, Dow Mossman, which didn't ring any bells. Then I read the title: *The Stones of Summer*. Tears began to well in my eyes, followed by full-on sobbing when I turned to the first page to find that it had been signed by the author.

Why did I cry when given a book first published in 1972 (when I was a toddler), which had been out of print for decades, written by an American author hardly anyone has ever heard of?

Many years ago, I went to see a documentary at the Sydney Film Festival, called *The Stone Reader*, by Mark Moskowitz. This particular movie wasn't my choice (I am not too fond of documentaries) but had been picked by my festival buddy. It turned out to be one of the best documentaries I have ever seen. I went home and told John the story from beginning to end, and couldn't stop talking about it for weeks. Perhaps it resonated so deeply with me because I am passionate about books – fiction in particular – and about writing. And this was a film about both.

The film documented the search for Dow Mossman, who, after publishing *The Stones of Summer* in 1972, vanished from the face of earth. The search took two years. When Moskowitz was initially unable to find him, the documentary became an exploration of Moskowitz's own lifelong relationship with books, and an examination of other classic 'one-off' novels – such as *The Catcher in the Rye* and *To Kill a Mockingbird*.

These days, both readers and publishers seem to expect authors to churn out dozens of books in a lifetime; but there are many authors who only ever wrote one complete book. Moskowitz cited a long list.

Why was Moskowitz obsessed with finding this virtually unknown author who hadn't written anything since the 1970s?

In 1972, Moskowitz, aged 18, rushed to buy *The Stones of Summer*, inspired by a review he had read in the *New York Times Book Review*. The reviewer, John Seelye, was one of many critics highly praising the book, comparing the first-time author to James Joyce, Mark Twain, JD Salinger, Philip Roth, and other writers of similar calibre. At the time, Moskowitz found the book 'impenetrable' and gave up after 20 pages. A quarter of a century passed before he picked it up again, when he was catching a plane and didn't have anything else to read. Now in his 40s, he was blown away by what he read. When he tried to find other works by this author, he discovered that Mossman hadn't published anything else, not even an article, in the past 30 years. So he set out to find him, to ask him why.

After travelling extensively, interviewing people (including John Seelye) who he thought might have clues that would lead him to Mossman, Moskowitz did eventually find his 'hero', still in Cedar Rapids, Iowa, where he had lived all his life. His one and only novel, which took him 10 years to write, had squeezed everything out of him – he'd had a breakdown after finishing the book and had ended up in a mental health facility. He never recovered fully; for the intervening 30 years, he worked as a truck driver, a welder, and when Moskowitz found him, he was ill with diabetes and wrapping newspapers for a living.

I remember shedding tears then, sitting in the theatre, watching the interview between Moskowitz and Mossman. To witness the devastating effect this writer's own creation had had on him, made worse by the poor sales of the book. Usually, it is the critics who have the power to destroy authors, but they had all raved about *Stones*. Still, the public did not 'get it'; Moskowitz himself abandoned it after a few pages, although he kept it on his shelf for a later date. I think the film also had a powerful effect on me because at the time I was struggling to formulate the beginnings of my first (and so far, only) novel, dealing with a recent diagnosis of diabetes and some mental health issues to boot.

As many of the filmgoers who watched *The Stone Reader* did, I assumed that *The Stones of Summer*, which had been out of print for three decades, would become widely available after the success of the award-winning documentary. I searched high and low in bookshops for several years, to no avail.

Eventually, I forgot about it – but John didn't.

'It's nothing short of amazing,' I said to John, when we finished exchanging gifts (yes, there were more gifts!). 'That after such an epic quest, Moskowitz found Mossman in the very town where he was born.'

'Wait a minute,' John interrupted. 'Where did you say the author lives?'

'Cedar Rapids, Iowa.'

'That's where the merchant I bought it from is based!' John exclaimed. 'Your book came from Cedar Rapids, Iowa.'

And that set me off crying again.

The Ideal Staycation

If you drive past my place, which is on one of the busiest roads in Sydney, you wouldn't suspect that there are two gateways to the bush within walking distance of that river of traffic. These are the Lane Cove National Park and the Berowra Valley Regional Park, each with intricate networks of bush tracks that open up in all directions. Some stretch hundreds of kilometres north, to Newcastle, others 30 kilometres south, to the city. Others wind through the creeks, gullies, valleys and heights of the local bushland, with its giant gum trees, lush ferns, makeshift bridges, rocky staircases and sandstone overhangs.

I have been living in the area for 20 years and over time, I have explored many of these tracks, sometimes alone, and sometimes with company. I have taken wrong paths a few times, I have started on one track and ended up on another, or lost the trail altogether and emerged in the streets. Notwithstanding my lack of sense of direction, as soon as I enter the bush, I am overcome by a sense of tranquillity. Smelling the eucalyptus trees, hearing the frogs and the birds chirping, the kookaburras laughing, the wind rustling the leaves and the water flowing in the creeks. Feeling the branches breaking and the pebbles crunching under my feet, and occasionally catching the sight of a lizard or bush turkey.

During the second year of the COVID-19 pandemic, I took annual leave for two weeks and it turned into a walking holiday in my own neighbourhood. I had booked a short trip away with my partner, and planned to have several catch ups with friends and family, which I always do around my birthday. However, Greater Sydney went into lockdown due to an outbreak of the Delta strain of COVID-19 just before I was due to take my leave, and all plans had to be cancelled.

So I made a long list of things to do during my break, from tasks such as wiping the hard drive of my old computer, to preparing my tax papers; projects that ranged from writing a blog post to reading at least two books; treats such as sleeping in every day and having a long, relaxing bath; and a challenge: to do 14 different walks in the 14 days of my break, of five to seven kilometres each.

Every morning during those two weeks, I set off after a late breakfast, feet clad in hiking shoes and walking pole in hand, and walked for up to two hours. In my travels, I discovered tracks and fire trails I didn't know existed, revisited paths I haven't walked for over a decade, completed walks I have been wanting to do for years, and hiked familiar, well-trodden paths I have done many times before. I saw the city from the lookout near Lorna's Pass, caught a glimpse of a wallaby hopping down one of the nearby hills, and snapped a photo of the Whale Rock in Devlin's Creek. Amazingly, I did not get lost once.

I also walked the steep streets of my neighbourhood, finding a secret community garden, hidden passageways, and brief corridors of bush behind the houses. I was blessed with great weather for walking. It was windy but sunny, and in 14 days I only wore my rain gear once, though the grey skies never opened. I couldn't go very far – we could not travel beyond 10 kilometres from home – but having a walking holiday for two weeks, even if it was in my own backyard, qualified as a 'dream holiday' for me.

During the pandemic, walking was my salvation. When we had to start working from home, throughout the nation-wide lockdown, I didn't take to it immediately. I missed the interaction with my colleagues, and the minimum of five kilometres I covered every day, walking to and from train stations, and sometimes walking all the way home from the office, which is six kilometres away. The walk was not as spectacular as crossing the Sydney Harbour Bridge, which I used to do every day after work when my office was based in the city; but it had seven steep hills that used to increase my heart rate and make the endorphins flow.

On my very first day of working from home in March 2020, I only walked a few hundred metres, and mostly in the corridors of my apartment building because it was pouring outside. I promised myself I would not let that happen again, and every day, no matter how busy I was, how low my mood or how bad the weather, I got out of my home office and walked. Sometimes I did it in three bursts – mid-morning, lunchtime and after work, which meant that in winter I had to walk in the dark. Walking got me out of my head, and helped dissipate the worries and uncertainty caused by the pandemic.

I have never been very adventurous or sporty, but have always been an avid walker. Growing up in the city of La Paz,

Bolivia, with its congested streets and haphazard public transport system, I used to walk everywhere. The CBD was only five kilometres from my house (as opposed to 30 kilometres in Sydney) and it was quicker to walk there than to wait for a bus that arrived packed to the brim, with a few people hanging on for their lives on the outside steps. This was decades before they installed a sophisticated cable car system, which has improved transportation enormously – something I only had the opportunity to experience in 2023 when the world opened up again and I dared to take my first international trip. Back in the 1980s, still in Bolivia, I would walk to university, in the southern suburbs, and to the conservatorium of music in the heart of the city. But all these walks were strictly urban.

Bushwalking is something I started doing more seriously when I had been living in Sydney for nearly two decades. I bought a book called *Sydney's Best Bush, Park & City Walks*, which took me to all corners of my adopted city, as I explored the walks with my partner or friends, methodically ticking them off as I went. I then moved on to another book, *Sydney's Best Harbour & Coastal Walks*. Soon after that, I attempted my first multi-day walk, the Milford Track in New Zealand, with a friend. I have since done the Inca Trail in Peru, the Three Capes Track in Tasmania, parts of the Great Ocean Walk in Victoria, and the last 120 kilometres of the Camino de Santiago in Spain.

At the end of my walking holiday, I thanked my lucky stars for living where I do, where I don't even have to drive to enter the magical world of the bush. I also thanked them for having two feet that take me places, far and near, with my footsteps often in sync with those of my friends.

Let this Moment Linger

There are the trivial questions in life, and then there are the big questions. What is the meaning of life? Why are we all here? What will I leave to the world when I'm gone? Will there be a moment, however brief, when I will understand it all?

According to legend, Faust exchanged his soul with the devil, Mephistopheles, so he could have a moment, just one moment, in which he would experience the highest, most amazing pleasure attainable by man. A moment so special, that he would want it to last forever.

Faust was, however, a difficult customer; no matter what Mephistopheles offered him – wealth, youth, knowledge, the love of no other than Helen of Troy, he remained unsatisfied. Finally, when he was an old man in his 80s, he found his 'moment' without Mephistopheles' help, when he stopped looking for his own happiness and found a way to give happiness to others.

Like Faust, I've often found myself searching for that transcendental experience that will change my life. I spent decades overlooking the present, waiting for that momentous revelation.

In an effort to focus on the here and now, I tried a number of techniques, including meditation and yoga. But my mind always raced ahead, worrying, searching, working things out, dealing with issues and scenarios that may never come to be.

ॐ

A few years ago, facing a change of circumstances that had been causing me a degree of anxiety, I was introduced to the practice of mindfulness, defined by Jon Kabat-Zin in his book *Whenever You Go, There You Are* (1994) as 'Paying attention in a particular way: on purpose, in the present moment, and non-judgmentally.' This sounds too simple, and it is. Ever since, whenever I can, I have been trying to pay attention to everything around me – focusing on what I can hear, what I can see, what I can feel, what I can smell, what I can taste. Trying to discover things in ordinary situations that I haven't noticed before. If I have stray thoughts, I observe them without judgement, and let them go.

A walk in the rain, an hour – or three – spent cleaning, or a short drive have suddenly transformed into special moments since I have been paying attention. Music has always had a way of heightening experiences for me; I now switch it off, so I can listen to the sounds around me: so many different birds chirping, the wind among the leaves, a plane in the distance, the constant flow of traffic on the busy road nearby, which after a while begins to sound like a river. Sometimes I even switch the light off when I'm having a shower – it is amazing how much you need to concentrate in the present moment when you don't have the luxury of sight – especially when you are shaving your legs!

One Easter Friday, my then partner John and I watched the 1957 movie *The Seventh Seal*, directed by the formidable Ingmar Bergman. The story takes place at Easter, during the Black Death (bubonic plague). Death is going around, having a field day, taking people right, left and centre. When he tries to sneak upon a knight who is returning from the Crusades, the knight challenges him to a game of chess, in an effort to prolong his life for a while. Knowing that all he has done is buy a little time, the knight wants to know that his life has had meaning; that all the years spent on the Crusades fighting for his God have been worth it, that there is something waiting for him after death – heaven or hell, it doesn't matter, as long as there is *something*. He asks these questions to a priest, to Death, to his God, even to a witch about to be burned at the stake, but the answers don't come.

He then meets a couple of itinerant artists, who are travelling with their baby. They offer him all they have – some music, freshly picked strawberries and a bowl of milk. Casting his internal struggle aside, the knight rejoices in that moment, saying he will remember that hour of peace. The strawberries, the bowl of milk, their faces in the dusk.

I now realise I don't want to wait until I'm 80 to experience 'my moment'. I don't want to sell my soul to the devil, or bargain with death in exchange for that transcendental experience.

If there's one thing I am beginning to understand, is that I no longer want to understand the meaning of life. I want instead to understand the meaning of each moment in my life. Because the secret is not in that one momentous revelation, that might never come, but in each single moment that makes our life, and which we so often dismiss as inconsequential.

I remember, for instance, the sense of satisfaction felt recently, after finishing a 10-kilometre walk with a friend. We were sitting at a café overlooking Narrabeen Lagoon on the northern beaches of Sydney, with sore muscles and gratified hearts, rewarding ourselves with a well-deserved meal. It was that 'in-between' time; too late for lunch and too early for dinner, and the place, usually busy, had a relaxed atmosphere enhanced by the laid-back music emanating from their sound system.

From my viewpoint, I could see the light of the afternoon sun reflected on the surface of the lagoon, kayakers floating peacefully on the waters, bikes zooming past, couples strolling, children laughing as they fed the ducks. And I thought – this is what life is all about: this moment.

Yesterday my 'moment' presented itself while I was driving to meet with friends to see a movie, when I witnessed a glorious sunset.

When all is said and done, if we can look back and remember the moments spent enjoying a good book, writing a poem, or gardening with the sun on our backs; and the moments of laughter, of joy and even of tears shared with lovers, family and friends, then we can say we have lived a life filled with happiness.

Today, my moment starts right here, right now, sharing my innermost thoughts with you, my reader. And to you, I say... let this moment linger!

PART 2:
PURPLE BUTTERFLY
SELECTED FICTION

Purple Butterfly

The clock radio comes on at 5.30 am, in the middle of the weather report. It snatches Jake out of the depths of sleep with predictions of another cold, cloudy winter's day with intermittent showers. With eyes tightly shut, he hits the 'snooze' button and tries, in vain, to catch the tail of his unfinished dream. It had been a good dream, a pleasant dream, but apart from that, he can't remember anything about it now that it's gone.

'Up, or you'll be late again,' Rose mumbles, elbowing him in the ribs. Having done her duty, she turns over and goes back to sleep; she has another 15 minutes.

Reality in all its ghastliness greets Jake from the dressing table mirror when he turns on the light. He has dark rings under the eyes, a beard growth of several days, and his flannelette pyjamas are so ragged even Vinnies would reject them. The man in the mirror looks at least a decade older than Jake's 30 years.

'I've been working in and out of the bloody rain for three days in a row,' Jake says, turning his back on reality. 'If it's like this tomorrow, I'm taking a sickie.'

'You can't, Jake. You ran out of sick leave,' Rose answers

from under the blankets. 'Besides, you shouldn't complain about the rain, with the drought and all.'

'Yeah, right.' Jake grunts and heads towards the shower, dragging his feet.

☙

J.R. Walters wakes up with a start, escaping from a nightmare. He looks at his watch: it's 5.30 a.m. With a shaky hand, he turns on his bedside lamp, lighting a bedroom that looks like a photograph in a lifestyle magazine.

'What's wrong?' his wife exclaims, sitting up in bed as if propelled by a spring.

But J.R. doesn't answer. He's busy checking the surroundings, making sure he's in his own room, in his house, not in a one-bedroom rented flat with mould-stained ceilings and second-hand furniture. He feels the texture of his pyjamas, and is reassured by the smoothness of silk. He runs his fingers over his chin, almost as smooth as his pyjamas. It was a dream, nothing but a dream.

'J.R., are you alright?' his wife asks again, scrunching up her eyes. Everybody calls him by his initials.

'Oh, I just had a dreadful nightmare!' J.R. says, breathing easier. 'And it felt so real!'

'Really? What about?'

He turns around to tell her about his dream, just in time to catch her yawning.

'Never mind. I'm okay now,' he says instead.

'In that case,' she says, 'I'm going back to sleep. Busy day today.'

'Yeah? What are you up to?'

'Mmm. Let's see. Riding lesson at ten, meeting Jane for a late lunch, and after school I'm taking the kids to their English tutor. It's Wednesday, remember?'

'Yes, I remember. I have a board meeting tonight, and tomorrow I'm off to Singapore.'

'Then, you should go back to sleep too,' she says, sliding back under the doona.

But J.R. is too awake and too shaken to sleep. He gets up and puts on a pair of slippers and a robe.

'I'm going for a walk; see if I can catch the sunrise,' he says to his wife, who responds with a series of gentle, regular snuffles.

℘

The sight of Rose's hands, fluttering all over the kitchen counter preparing sandwiches for lunch, brings back a residue of Jake's dream to the foreground of his mind.

'There was a butterfly,' he says, thinking aloud.

'Last time I checked, it wasn't a butterfly yet,' Rose answers, as if she knows exactly what he's talking about.

'What?' Jake says, forehead furrowed.

'You mean the cocoon outside, don't you? The one we saw when we came home yesterday. I had a look this morning, while you were getting dressed, and it's still there, and it's still a cocoon. It's so bloody cold, I hope it survives.'

'Oh, the cocoon. No wonder I dreamed of butterflies,' Jake says, and then he closes his eyes, delving deep into his subconscious. There was a butterfly at the very end, but before... and then poof! He remembers some more. 'Yes!'

'What?' Rose says, half-hearing. She's busy cutting up

the sandwiches in triangles and wrapping them in plastic. She's unaccustomed to early morning conversations on weekdays; there's never enough time.

'I just remembered a dream I had last night,' Jake says. 'A pretty cool one, too!'

'Yeah? What about?' Rose puts down the knife to give Jake her undivided attention.

'I dreamed we were loaded,' he gets up and paces around the kitchen, waving his hands. He's wearing navy-blue overalls and workmen's boots. 'We lived in a mansion, with a pool and all, we had two kids and a maid. I flew business class all over the joint, and all you had to do all day was ride horses, socialise and take the kids to private tutors.'

'Ride horses? Ha!' Rose exclaims, sweeping the air with her hand and going back to her sandwiches. 'Fancy that! If I could afford not to work, I can think of a million things better to do than ride horses.'

છ

J.R. stands outside his house, shivering slightly although he's thrown a navy overcoat on top of his robe. It is still dark outside and he doesn't think he'll be able to withstand the cold until the sun finally decides to come up. He's leaning on a concrete rubbish bin and smoking a cigarette while he waits. His wife thinks he quit long ago, but he still sneaks one here and there. Just then, a garbage collection truck approaches noisily, casting an eerie glow upon the half-lit street. A garbo gets off and walks towards J.R. – or rather, towards the concrete bin on which he's leaning.

'G'day! You mind? I'm all out of matches,' the garbo says,

taking a packet of cigarettes out of his pocket with a gloved hand. J.R. hesitates for a second but lights up the garbo's cigarette. They both lean on the bin, exhaling smoke.

'It's a hard life, hey, mate? Us having to start work at the crack of dawn while the snobs in this street are still dreaming.'

J.R. nods in agreement, amused.

'But you know what?' the garbo says, 'I might be a wog, and a garbo, but I wouldn't wanna trade places with any of the poor sods that live here.'

J.R. looks at the garbo with raised eyebrows. He's afraid that if he opens his mouth and speaks with the careful elocution he was taught in private school, the garbo will discover he's been smoking with the enemy. The garbo leans towards him.

'See, my cousin's a gardener, and he's got a few clients in this street,' he says, almost in a whisper. 'He tells me that half the missuses here are screwing their personal trainers or riding instructors, 'cause their hubbies are never home.'

He pauses, for effect, and to take another puff of his ciggie.

'Get it? Riding instructors,' the garbo says, rocking his pelvis. At this, he cracks into roaring laughter, waiting for J.R. to join him. Instead, J.R. breaks into a coughing fit.

'You right there, mate?' the garbo says, stubbing his cigarette in the bin, and patting J.R. on the back.

'I'll be right,' J.R. manages to say when he's recovered. 'You carry on with your work.'

'Okay then. Ta for the light!'

When the garbo is gone, J.R. notices that a purple butterfly has appeared out of nowhere and it settles on his left shoulder. He flicks it off and shuffles back to his door, shaking his head, just as the sun rises amidst the clouds.

CB

The first rays of sunlight slip through the blinds in the kitchen, forcing Jake to close his eyes. When he opens them again, the first thing he sees is his wife, standing in front of the window, still in her nightdress, glowing like a rough diamond. She's handing him a plastic bag with his lunch. Instead of taking the bag, Jake takes Rose in his arms, and kisses her on the neck.

'Wow. What brought THAT on?' Rose says.

'I just remembered the rest of the dream,' Jake says, peering at the clock over Rose's shoulder. It's 6.30 am. 'Crap! I'm going to miss the bus again!'

He grabs his lunch and toolbox and races towards the door, with Rose racing behind.

'Hon, don't forget I've got Tech tonight. But dinner's in the fridge; just needs five minutes on medium-high,' Rose says, stepping outside.

The sun has fully risen in a silvery blue sky. The garbo emptying the bins outside their block of flats waves at them, and they wave back.

Rose kisses her husband lightly on the lips with her eyes half-open.

'Hey, look!' She jumps, pointing towards the bush behind Jake. The cocoon is in the process of opening, and a glorious purple butterfly breaks free, unfolding its wings in slow motion. 'Ain't that amazing?'

'Never seen anything so beautiful, babe,' Jake says,

already jogging to the bus stop, followed by the newborn butterfly.

A few people, all blue-collar workers, wait for the bus, which is just turning the corner. As he joins the queue, Jake realises that the gloominess he felt upon waking has dissipated along with the rain.

21 Years

There he was, in front of her, packing his bags. Looking somewhat forlorn and at the same time, so determined, that if it weren't for her own resentment, her desperation, she would have rushed in to help him. She would lay down his clothes, just like she did every time he was about to set on a trip: Look, take these socks – they match better with that shirt; fold that carefully, I just ironed it; get the other suitcase, that one is too small...

Twenty-one years, she thought, while bitter teardrops threatened to burst from her eyes. For 21 years I stayed behind, here, isolated, so that you could get ahead. I missed the world so that you could gain it, expecting your sporadic presents – sometimes a dress, other times a night out to the movies – as if they were the only blessings in my life. Not seeing, or not wanting to see that those gifts were, at least, what I well deserved. I deserved that, and much more. And now, just like that, you pack your luggage and announce you're leaving?

They had shared so many things together, in that place. She was always cooking for him, knitting jumpers for him, mending his clothes. And he was always discontented, never satisfied. Not so much with her, but with life.

'But… don't you understand?' he said. 'That there has to be something beyond all this, the four walls of this house, the small streets of this outer suburb? We are here to do much more; surely we can't be happy for the simple fact that we exist, here and now? Can't you see a little bit beyond the daily routine?'

'No, Raphael,' she would argue, 'I can't see a thing. Isn't my love enough for you, and all the things I give you? You're all I need.'

She often wondered if his dissatisfaction stemmed from the fact they had come to live in this country, so far away from the place they were born. It was also true that often she felt she didn't belong here, but as long as they were together, it didn't trouble her as much as it troubled him.

'If love, as you think, were enough for everything… oh, can't you see?' he would say, adamantly peering over his book. 'Then, we could sit at the table, to eat love, to drink love, to chew and breathe love. Even happiness itself is only an illusion.'

Yes, Raphael, she answered, this time in silence. Always talking to me as if I didn't have a brain, as if I were crawling light years behind you. But what you don't know is that I also have the capacity to decide, and make choices. As I did last Tuesday, only last Tuesday, and what else do you want! I chose you and would choose you again.

☙

That Tuesday morning, three knocks on the door surprised her before she was ready. She finished applying the lipstick, and even though this scene had been repeated every second Tuesday for years, her hand was still shaking when she turned the knob. The man embraced her and slipped inside in silence.

Afterwards, on the still unmade bed, he had taken her face in his hands, forcing her to look into his eyes.

'How much longer, Adele? How much longer are we going to wait? Any day now I'm going to run into my fiftieth birthday and I'll still be coming here, like a thief, to knock on your door once a fortnight. Like two kids playing naughty games. I want you to move in with me. When are you going to think about yourself?'

'You know I can't. It would be such a shock to Raphael.'

'Why don't you let me talk to him?'

She shook her head, her eyes wide.

'No, no. I'm the one who has to do it. But I can't...'

'In that case, you better call me when you make up your mind. Call me, Adele, and when you do, I will come to take you away with me there and then. But don't expect me back until that day.'

☘

She had let him go, just like that. And she had said nothing about it to Raphael or anyone else. Nor did she say a word when she saw Raphael one day last April, one of the few times she'd ventured out all the way to Pitt Street Mall, in the city.

She saw him sitting on a bench outside Myer, next to a young woman. They were both laughing so heartily – clearly, he wasn't telling her the things he always told Adele about the futility of life...

Adele said nothing; she didn't even approach them. With a knot in her stomach, she just retraced her tracks and went home. That night she waited, to see if he said anything, if something in his expression divulged a clue.

Yet he gave nothing away. She could understand that he wouldn't tell her other things; for example, that the earrings he'd given her, saying they were gold, were not. Mr Martin the jeweller had remarked upon it without guile, when she went to get them cleaned.

But, if he was seeing this young woman, who made him laugh like she never saw him laugh in their house… that, at least, after all the years that they spent together, she deserved to know.

♣

And that's how she found herself that Friday, leaning against the doorframe of that room, watching him while he packed, without telling her that he was leaving until then. Leaving her for a woman whose name she didn't even know.

'You knew it would have to be like this,' said Raphael, still packing. 'Sooner or later, it had to be this way. I know what's best for you and for me. Maybe she isn't exactly what's lacking in my life, but she's willing to go wherever we need to go in order to find it. At least I know I can make her happy. That's enough reason to begin with.'

Finally, she found her voice. It came out in a cascade of emotions, surprising her more than him.

'And now you tell me all this? After the 21 years I denied myself the right to live, only for you? Now, you take all the clothes that I sewed for you and take off with a girl so young she probably doesn't even know how to thread a needle? Is this the way you leave?'

He paused for a moment, deep in thought. Then his features softened and at last he spoke in a gentler tone, with a newly discovered intimacy.

'Do you honestly believe that I would leave without knowing that there's someone also waiting for you, and whose only obstacle is me? Why don't you want to understand that this is also the chance to get on with your own life?'

Tears in her eyes dried up instantly, as the truth finally rumbled in her ears for the first time: That's right, damn it, I can also be happy without Raphael! But she said nothing. Instead, she left the room.

When she came back from the kitchen, he was waiting with his suitcase in the doorway.

'Take these,' she said, giving him two small packages. 'One is a slice of the apple pie I made today. Take it for the road. And here... here's some money I had saved in case of an emergency. No, don't turn it down; I know that look of rejection in your eyes only too well. Take it – you're going to need it more than I am. Aren't you going to give me a goodbye kiss?'

He hugged her lovingly and gave her a kiss on the cheek.

'Everything will be all right, Mum. You know it's for the best.'

'Go, my son, I think you may be right. Today is a new beginning in our lives. Both yours and mine.'

Go, Raphael, go! she thought. For 21 years, from the day you were born, I saw through your eyes, spoke through your mouth, worked through your hands. Now you're leaving, and I'm left with the sad and surprising fact that I have hands, and a mouth and eyes of my own. Maybe I still have enough time to learn to use them.

She watched Raphael from the window, and sighed when he turned the corner. Only then she picked up her phone and called, with resolve, with hope, with a new smile growing in her spirit, that familiar number.

After George

You are sitting in the darkness, waiting. Through the window the neon lights of the shops give the room an eerie atmosphere, but the familiar chords from 'Wish You Were Here' by Pink Floyd help dissipate the unease you are feeling.

You have been dating Mike for several weeks and this is the first time that you agree to come upstairs for a nightcap. After gulping down a glass of his Scotch, he goes into the bathroom to have a shower and asks you to make yourself comfortable. The only thing you can think of is to find the switch and turn the light off. You are as nervous as you had been on your first time. Well, it *is* your first time with him.

After George exited your life, you have been dating a parade of guys of all nationalities, sizes and professions for months on end, but none of them have got this far. Perhaps you are getting tired of this quest for the perfect successor?

You feel like one of those people you interview at the employment agency, who have been working in the same company for decades and all of a sudden get retrenched. They keep coming back to see you every time there is a vacancy in their field, because after all those years of stability they don't seem to be able to find a steady job.

After seven years together, George retrenched you. He found someone more suitable. Good for him. And you? Well, you were caught unawares and discovered that this business of being in the 'meet market' again was rather terrifying. Damn George, you think. Damn George. Damn the agency too. It makes you assess your lovers as if they were candidates for a job.

You hear a crash and Mike swearing under his breath. He has knocked something over – a chair. You can out make his silhouette, crouching, grabbing the foot he's just hurt.

'Julie?' he calls. 'You still there?'

'Over here, on the couch.'

'What happened to the lights? I nearly broke my toe!' he says, limping his way towards the couch.

'I like it dark.' You try to sound seductive and relaxed, but a quiver in your voice betrays you.

'Oh, well. I may be limping, but I'm still fully functional.'

You start giggling. He always makes you laugh.

His is a tiny bachelor flat with the view of a busy street. You have learned a few things about Mike: you know he owns this studio apartment; you know he works in the car park, inside a little glass cage, where he reads science fiction novels and listens to Pink Floyd all day. You have seen him there, every day, for months, ever since you started working in that building. You know he is kind of shy. It must have taken him a lot of courage to wait for you outside his booth that night, a couple of months ago.

'Hi,' he had said, 'I was wondering, if you had nothing better to do, maybe you'd like to come and see a movie with me sometime?'

The following Friday you had gone to see the latest instalment of *Star Wars* with him, and you hadn't minded it at all, even though you hadn't seen the other two prequels. You have to admit you don't mind science fiction, and you like Pink Floyd. That's a start.

You know he is kind of cute, and two years younger than you. He is down to earth and laid back, maybe too much so. But then again, George was too complicated – everything, even grocery shopping, was a mind-boggling affair when you were with him.

You like the little you know about Mike, but he could be a closet psycho for all you know. He had to ask several times before you agreed to come upstairs.

Without warning, he nibbles your neck, making you jolt. Then your shoulders, your arms, your earlobes. You are beginning to enjoy yourself, despite the crazy thoughts that race through your mind. The earlobes? George never did that, you think. You try to switch your brain off, to expunge George's ghost from the room. When Mike starts kissing your belly, and works his way up to your breasts, you finally begin to relax and with your hands and lips find his naked shoulders, his neck. He smells of Imperial Leather and he seems to know your body in a way George never did.

Hours later, the thin light of dawn filters through the blinds and you take stock of the subtle mess surrounding you. Clothes are scattered all over the floor and the chair is still lying on its side, right where it fell. Your nightcap is sitting on the coffee table, untouched. You both fell asleep on the couch but at some point, Mike must have rolled down onto the floor. The sight of him sprawled on the carpet makes you chuckle.

Suddenly, you realise you can't even remember what's-his-name's face.

You tap Mike on the shoulder – he opens one eye and smiles. Unabashed, you let him see you, naked in the light of the day. You slide to the floor and, climbing on top of him, this time you take the initiative.

This short story was originally published in *Verandah Literary Journal* Volume 23, Faculty of Arts, Deakin University, Victoria, Australia, 2008.

Tears in the Wind

On Valentine's Day, while sweeping the platforms at the railway station just before the end of her shift, Matilda couldn't help but notice a handsome guy sitting on one of the benches. He was wearing a business suit, silk tie and shiny black shoes, and was holding a bouquet of red roses. He'd been there for a while but didn't get on any of the trains. He just sat there, presumably waiting for his girl to arrive, but she never did.

Something caught Matilda's eye: a tear trickled down his face, glistening in the afternoon sun. Another followed. He had the saddest and prettiest blue eyes, she thought, if a little bloodshot. Matilda wondered how long he'd been sitting there with his crimson flowers, his polished shoes and his shiny cheeks, waiting. She had never seen a grown man cry in public, alone, making no effort to hide his emotions. She ran to the ticket office and pointed him out to her colleague Priya.

'Do you think they broke up? Perhaps he was planning to propose tonight, and she ran away with someone else!' said Matilda, letting her imagination run wild.

Priya just rolled her eyes and went back to her post at

the ticket window. Matilda's tendency to dramatise every-thing was like a centrifugal force that made her common sense spin until there was nothing left of it. And she was a hopeless romantic to boot.

They had been working together at that busy train station for nearly three years. Even though Priya was seven years younger than Matilda, they had formed a strong bond through their shared toils. They had emptied rubbish bins, washed walls and mopped floors together – and often had to clean up the mess that the drunk crowds made on Friday nights, when they threw up their guts in the middle of the platform. There was nothing romantic about that.

They had been abused by commuters when the trains were late or cancelled, even though it was clearly not their fault. And they were often treated as though they were stupid because they were doing a job that didn't require formal qualifications. This extended to Matilda's family, who could not accept that, at age 30, she was happy working as a train station attendant and had no desire to have a 'proper' career.

It was different in Priya's case, because she was only doing a few shifts to support herself while she studied a distance education degree. Because she was an immigrant and spoke with a heavy accent, people often thought that the best she could aspire to was a menial job. But she would soon be qualified to be a forensic psychologist.

Matilda, on the other hand, was the personification of an Anglo-Australian of Irish descent, with her red hair, fair skin and freckled face. She spoke impeccable English and towered over Priya as she stood in front of her in the small ticket office. She was witty and intelligent, yet she had dropped out of school in Year 10 and had worked in a series of dead-end jobs until she'd landed this position, which, despite all the toils and her family's reservations, she seemed to love. Appearances could be so deceiving.

Having second thoughts about ignoring Matilda's story about the crying man, Priya decided to feed her friend's fantasy even more.

'Or worse; what if...' Priya said, pausing for effect. 'what if his girlfriend was on her way here, but had an accident and died?'

'Oh, my God, how tragic!' Matilda said, getting teary herself. 'He thinks he's been stood up, and nobody has called him to tell him what happened.'

'If he's crying,' said Priya, 'maybe someone *has* told him.'

Sometime later, when Matilda went home, the poor fellow was still there, still weeping. His image stayed in her mind's eye long after she left the station.

A few days later, she spotted his face in the peak-hour crowd on the platform. More than anything, she immediately recognised his baby-blue eyes. This time he was wearing jeans and a torn T-shirt, and instead of roses he was carrying a battered backpack. How different he looked in that outfit! He was standing against the wall, chatting with two other young men his age. He was chuckling at a joke one of his mates made.

The distinct sparkle of a tear caught Matilda's attention, before he quickly wiped it with the back of his hand, and kept on talking. She realised he wasn't crying; he never had been. He just had some condition that made for watery eyes.

Simone's First Prank
(or Snakeman in Paris)

Before moving to Sydney, where my husband Jean-Pierre and I perform jazz and bossa nova at a nightclub at Bondi, we lived here in Paris for some time. This is where our daughter Simone, whom we affectionately call Moni, was conceived and born. The embodiment of multiculturalism, she is a bilingual French–Australian with olive skin, copper hair, her father's blue eyes and the high cheekbones of my people.

I was a newcomer in Paris when, a few minutes after midday on a hot Wednesday afternoon, I passed out right over there, on the corner of La Cour de Rome and Gare Saint-Lazare. That was the day we found out I was pregnant, and Jean-Pierre never gets tired of telling the story of what he calls 'Simone's first prank' to anyone who will listen.

But before Paris and long before Bondi, I used to live in a picturesque neighbourhood in yet another continent; where the narrow, uneven streets were paved with mud and stones. My city of birth was full of contradictions: young and old, rich and poor, the holy and the profane, all blended in this place at the heart of South America. There, people were still in contact with the extraordinary aspects of ordinary living, with the day-to-day magic of existence.

And it was there that I believe the story of my fainting in Paris began, long before Moni was conceived. With the conviction of my people, I trust the version I'm about to tell, more than Jean-Pierre's rational explanation of Parisian heat and morning sickness.

In my South American days, I wasn't a jazz singer. In fact, I was – well, was aspiring to be – a classical concert pianist. I was also a consummate dreamer; a quality I hope I still possess. But even in my wildest teenage dreams, I had not visualised that one day, almost overnight, I would be living in Paris, making music alongside my French husband.

It wouldn't have been three months since we'd carried my few belongings into Jean-Pierre's bachelor apartment on the third floor at 13 Rue Crémieux. I was about to cross the street, on my way to meet him at this café, when I fell flat on my back and lost consciousness. Fortunately, Jean-Pierre was already sitting here, probably at this very table. I can picture him, bored to death, casually yet impatiently scanning the crowds while he yawned for the hundredth time.

We had arranged to meet at 11.30 am. As usual, I was running late. I have lost count of how many times I've tried to explain to my husband the concept of Latin-American time: always half an hour to one hour later than agreed. But to this day, he's still operating by the European clock. That's why he always carries a book in his pocket when we are meeting.

Back then, he hadn't yet developed a taste for reading, and as soon as he saw the commotion across the road, he approached the crowd to find out what was going on. Although I could not contaminate him with my unpunctuality, the typical curiosity of Latin people was something we had in common. To his dismay it was me, sprawled out on the pavement, who was attracting the attention of the passers-by gathered opposite Le Concourse.

I woke up in hospital, with concussion and a very emotional Jean-Pierre sitting next to me. With a shaky voice, which made his Spanish almost unintelligible (my French was worse on a good day, so we still communicated in Spanish) he told me that the doctors had found out the reason for my 'accident'.

'*Estás embarazada!*' he blurted.

Yes, I was expecting a baby. What a fright she gave us! She announced herself in French style. Sirens, ambulance, everything. All we needed were fireworks.

And that's the official version of what Jean-Pierre always referred to as 'Simone's first prank'.

❧

However, Simone, my dramatic passing out that day was not your fault. In fact, it was simply a coincidence. Now that we are here, back in Paris, I can remember that day as if it were yesterday. Thirteen years in Sydney, living so close to the ocean, seeing you grow up with a surfboard under your arm, and us working at a nightclub on the beachfront, can make anyone forget so many things.

When I brought you here this morning, I thought of

telling you, 'Here, this is where I fainted and nearly broke my skull 16 years ago.' But now that we are at the actual location, there's so much more that comes to mind. Do you want to hear my version of the facts? I thought so.

How did I end up that day in Paris, with the brand-new name of Madame Durand, when only a couple of months earlier I was a single young woman who hadn't even left her grandparents' house in Sopocachi? I've asked myself that question many a time, in disbelief. And you already know a great deal of the answer, Moni. But I have to tell you again – I just love seeing you roll your eyes.

The night I met your father, I was with some friends at La Bohemia, a nightclub in Sopocachi. We were drowning our frustrations with copious amounts of piña colada. That very night I'd been dismissed as the accompanist of the university choir, because I had the cheek to challenge one of the conductor's decisions in front of the choristers. We were rehearsing for a production of *Carmen*.

My loyal friends Mariela and Katia saw what happened, and quit the choir on the spot. They wanted to make, if not a stand, at least a statement in the light of such injustice. We knew exactly what that meant for us: for at least six months, we'd made ourselves outcasts from any other musical production since he was – apart from being a pig – a very influential man. Mari and Katia didn't mind that much; they were not getting paid to sing.

The musical scene in our city was so small that everybody knew everybody and the news would spread like wildfire the next day. My livelihood didn't depend on this production; I still had my job teaching at the conservatorium.

My friends and I decided to do what we always did on such occasions, when rightful vindication was required: we made ourselves seen and heard publicly using our classically trained voices to sing 'profane' songs in dubious nightclubs.

I had just finished making a fool of myself singing 'Garota de Ipanema' in very bad Portuguese, when the keyboard player who accompanied me took me aside. In broken Spanish but with an exquisite French accent, he asked whether I was interested in singing jazz and bossa nova with him. He had just completed a contract in Brazil, where he'd split up with his partner, Genevieve. She'd fallen for her samba instructor, a *mulatto* who'd taught her to dance in ways she'd never thought possible.

I was stunned that he approached me, because in my opinion, Mari and Katia had much better voices. And I was primarily a pianist, not a singer. I was ready to tell the foreigner that jazz was not my type of music. But soon I remembered my recent operatic tragedy, and having had too many glasses of piña colada, I accepted his offer.

'So, less than a month later, Dad and you were on a plane on the way to Paris, where you tied the knot, leaving all your family and friends back home, speechless,' you say, finishing my sentence. You've heard this story so many times.

Speechless is a mild way of putting it, Moni. They were livid. They called your dad the 'French child molester' – I had just turned 21 and he was 35. Personally, I'd never dreamed of meeting a man as handsome and gentle as him. Much less that I'd fall in love with this blue-eyed angel with a French accent on the very night he had landed at La Bohemia.

A few weeks later, when your dad asked me to go back to Paris with him, I thought my leaving the country was the perfect revenge against the artistic elite of our hometown. I could yet have a chance at having a career in music; in fact, I saw myself as the feminine re-incarnation of Gershwin, 'a Latin-Americana in Paris'. Indeed, I envisaged nothing but a bright future, and didn't realise my family and friends would be so mad that they'd refuse to answer my letters or take my phone calls. Only Nana Dolores, your great-grandmother, who had died two years before any of this happened, was still speaking to me.

☙

That Wednesday in Paris, the day of your first prank, I'd boarded the 'S' bus minutes before noon. I could have walked but I was late – it was a bad decision. It was rush hour, when everybody is going home for lunch. I remember the first thing I thought was, *This bus reminds me so much of the buses back home*. Old and narrow, it looked as if it were about to collapse any minute under the weight of the commuters.

The odour of sweat, the lack of fresh air and the heat made me instantly dizzy. The only thing that was missing to make me feel completely at home were the solid indigenous women, dressed with ample *polleras*, bowler hats covering their thick, dark, braided hair, carrying their children wrapped in colourful fabrics on their backs. And, of course, the cold weather. How much was I missing the cool breeze that enveloped the Andean midday throughout the year!

The 'S' bus in Paris was completely packed with people of all shapes and colours. Everybody, the living and the dead, were on that bus. I had to travel the few blocks that separated me from the Cour de Rome on my feet, squeezed between two Frenchmen who didn't strike me as shy.

A young man standing nearby caught my eye. Despite the heat, he was wearing a black felt hat and an overcoat. He had an unusually long, elongated neck with a scar running from his chin to his chest, disappearing underneath the collar of his overcoat. I had to look away. He reminded me too much of the 'Snakeman' of our house in Sopocachi, whom my Nana used to terrify me with as a child.

⁊

One day, ma cherie, I'll take you to my old house in Sopocachi. It's double the size, and decades older than our townhouse at Bondi Beach. We'll have to go there soon, before you're old enough to feel ashamed to be seen travelling with your folks.

I have no idea who lives in that house these days. The property was sold after Nana died. The only inhabitant who I am sure is still there, is the Snakeman. Perhaps Nana Dolores and he can finally carry out a civilised conversation. They never had one when she was alive. He occupied the basement of our house long before Nana was born. She saw him several times, when she ventured down there to find something because they used the basement to store old paraphernalia.

'Are you telling me that she saw a—?' you interrupt, looking at me with round eyes.

Yes, Moni, she clearly saw him, although she could never see him up close. Whenever she tried to get near, he would vanish into the darkness. She could only catch a glimpse of his black silhouette, perhaps the reflection of his shadow on the walls.

She described him as a long, skinny man, wrapped up in a black overcoat and covering his head – which she imagined would be bald and slippery – with a black felt hat. She baptised him the Snakeman, or *Culebrón* in Spanish.

He must've liked Nana, for he never made himself seen by any other member of the family. The huge basement, seen through my child-eyes, resembled an enormous catacomb. It was the realm of my grandpa. He spent most of his afternoons there, where he'd set up a carpentry workshop to entertain the long hours of retirement.

He never came across the resident ghost, but he didn't mind either way. As he used to say, 'As long as that elusive character dressed in black doesn't interfere with me or my work, I'm quite happy to share the basement with another tenant.' Always so formal, Grandpa.

As a child, I couldn't find the nerve to go down the narrow staircase that led to the underground, unless someone else descended first and turned all the lights on for me. I was terrified of running into the Snakeman. My Nana discovered that I was frightened of her slippery friend and, ingenious as she was, took advantage of my phobia.

Every day, when I was small and stubbornly refused to eat my vegetables (and if they made me, I'd throw them up), Nana, the cheeky Señora Dolores, threatened to take me to the basement, where she'd leave me to the mercy of the Snakeman.

When I grew up, I found other interests – and fears – in life. I was more interested, for example, in classical music, the environment, and thanks to Nana, vegetarian food. And what terrified me beyond measure, were those strange creatures of the opposite sex who for some reason, seemed interested in me.

In fact, as the years went by, I started to feel sorry for the Snakeman. Both my grandparents were becoming too old to go down the dark, steep staircase to the basement, and he probably spent his days wandering in the darkness, feeling deserted and lonely.

During the years of my musical studies, the basement became my refuge. It was the only place in the house where I could play and listen to music as loud as I wanted without bothering anyone. I set up a small study, where I kept boxes of sheet music, my portable keyboard, a cassette player and, of course, a heater.

Many a time I imagined him, a silent spectator, sitting behind me, sheltered by the darkness. Deeply touched by the passionate arias of Puccini and the playful melodies of Mozart.

A phantom of the opera, condemned to eternal silence.

'You know, Simone? I could not conceive a greater punishment than silence. It would be like taking the sea away from you. What would you do if you couldn't swim or surf? Remember how you felt when we moved to the big house in the Hills Shire, where the closest beach was an hour's drive? You nearly went into depression, ma cherie! You were so relieved when we sold the house and moved back to Bondi, even though the town house was so much smaller. The same goes for me. My voice, my ability to sing, is what keeps me going in life... and you.'

'... and Dad.'

'... And Dad. The thing is, in time, I forgot all about the Snakeman...'

⌇

'Forgive me, ma cherie, I got sidetracked. But I had to give you the background to the Snakeman, so you know what I am talking about. Where was I?'

'On the 'S' bus, Ma. Here, in Paris.'

I must be getting homesick, I remember saying to myself, whilst I tried to ignore the insistent smile of the Frenchman who was squeezing me on the bus. The unexpected apparition of the Snakeman-look-alike on this bus, had brought to the foreground of my mind memories that I had long ago stored away. My house, my childhood, my grandmother, her wordless friendship with the Snakeman in our basement.

At that precise moment I also realised I'd only spoken to Nana the night before, in my dreams. She often visited me there, even more frequently since I'd moved to Paris. In this dream in particular, she'd come to tell me something like this: 'Dear, don't worry too much about losing your family. They will come back, like prodigal children, in due course. Now you must be strong, for you will have your own family to take care of.'

Nana. Even when alive she had a habit of speaking in riddles. But ever since she died, her language had become even more cryptic.

Somehow, I felt comforted by her words. Particularly

because she wasn't upset with me like everybody else, for running away to the other side of the world with a foreigner who almost doubled me in age. Indeed, Nana had become a lot more tolerant since she'd passed away.

The Snakeman on this bus brought me back from my reverie into the hot Parisian afternoon, when he had an argument with the man standing next to him. Back in those days I could hardly understand French, but his tone annoyed me straight away. He had a crybaby sort of voice that quickly became nasty. Fortunately, I realised it was my stop, and got off.

A few minutes later, I was in La Cour de Rome, across from the Gare St-Lazare, worried, thinking that Jean-Pierre must have given up and gone.

To my surprise, I heard the same annoying voice as before, right behind me. I turned around and there he was, the Snakeman-like person speaking with another man, who was telling him something while he pointed to the scar on his neck with the fat fingers of his only arm.

The second man looked as if he had just run away from a circus, a creature suitable for a Parisian child's nightmare. Although I could hardly understand, I caught a few words here and there: *bouton, manteau, cou...* I presumed the grotesque little character was telling the Snakeman that he should add another button to his overcoat, to hide the scar. All of a sudden, the Snakeman turned around, as if he'd felt my gaze upon him, and our eyes met. I looked away, frightened and dizzy.

I saw that your father was still waiting for me across the road, and relief washed over my body. Jean-Pierre was absorbed with the menu and hadn't seen me. But I never made it across the street. I was there in the corner, waiting for the lights to change, when I realised the Snakeman was beside me, almost touching my hand with his coated arm. He was also waiting for the green sign.

And I swear over Nana's grave, that the last thing I remember, before everything went black on the day of your first prank, is that the Snakeman of Paris looked at me straight in the eyes, his mouth curved in a toothless, ageless smile.

And then, in perfect Spanish, he whispered in my ear: *'Hola, Corazón. Comiste todas tus verduras hoy?'*

'Hello, sweetheart,' he said. 'Did you eat all your vegies today?'

It All Began with a Tulip

It all began with a tulip. There were also water lilies... but let me get back to the tulip.

It was a bright, saffron-yellow colour and you fastened it to my collar with a safety pin. You even thought of bringing a safety pin!

My mother wasn't impressed. She believed that when it came to flowers, yellow signified disdain. Reds, pinks, whites and all hues in between were perfectly fine, but yellow was the wrong colour if you wanted to make a good first impression on my mother.

She didn't say anything to you, though. She just watched us take off in your car (would you believe I don't remember what colour your car was, back in those days?) and she waved us goodbye with teeth clenched behind her smile.

Later that night, after you delivered me home, safe, sound and still a virgin, I pressed the tulip, which was already languishing, between the pages of the phone book.

Let's move on to the water lilies. It was a fine summer's afternoon on a lazy Saturday, two years after that first date. We were at a picturesque park near my house, featuring a pond at its heart. The dried tulip, together with the dried yellow roses and daffodils that came later, was by then living – or should I say perpetually dying – between the leaves of an old journal.

My mother continued to believe that your preference for yellow was a bad omen; if you held me in such contempt then, what would it be like after we got married, after we had children, after we became as used to each other as one does to wearing a pair of old, faded jeans?

She never voiced any of these concerns to you, though. She only brought them up with me, usually when we were alone in the sewing room, as she struggled in vain to teach me the art of dressmaking, to prepare me for married life. Much as I tried to please her, my patterns were always crooked and my stitches uneven.

To her despair, I was not nearly as interested in crafts as I was in numbers, and she blamed you for that too. On the formulas and equations you shared with me, the spreadsheets you taught me to create, your theories about measured risk-taking, about odds and percentages, about everything in life being subject to the laws of statistics.

She must have been right, because when you produced the ring from your pocket that particular Saturday afternoon, as you knelt down next to the pond, and asked me the question I never thought you would ask, I answered you with another question:

'What would you say are the odds of me saying yes?'

'I'd say 99 to one,' you answered confidently.

To your disbelief, I snatched the ring from your fingers and hurled it into the murky pond.

'Ha! And what do you think are the odds of you finding that ring in the pond?' I asked, but you were too stunned to reply. You stood up slowly, and stared hopelessly at the pond.

'Perhaps one in a million,' you managed to mumble when you found your voice. 'Have you any idea,' you then said, striving to sound calm, 'how many months' salary I spent on that ring?'

And with that, you turned on your heels and walked away.

Later, when I told my mother, she put down her knitting and marched to the pond in the park, with me speeding along behind her.

'The problem with that young man,' she said as we approached, 'is that he only believes in numbers, and there are times in life one needs to believe in miracles.'

And I watched my mother, my big old fleshy mother, strip down to her undergarments and disappear into the green, murky pond. She emerged at the centre, among the water lilies. There, resting on one of the leaves, catching the light of the dying sun, was the ring.

Teddy's Room

The day Wendy introduced Aurelia to her only child, the women had known each other for about eight months. Aurelia had moved to the cottage next door to Wendy's in the spring of 2035. They were both in their early sixties, although Wendy looked older than Aurelia because she'd allowed Mother Nature to take its course. Silver threads interlaced with her once-red hair, and wrinkles were evident around her mouth and eyes, particularly when she smiled. Aurelia, who had been a celebrity most of her life, had always looked the part, even after her retirement: her dyed-black hair carefully piled up on top of her head, impeccable attire and make up, and her skin as smooth as a baby's bottom, thanks to regular lifts.

Aurelia had no reason to think there was anything odd about her neighbour, except perhaps her extreme fascination with teddy bears. Wendy collected toy bears – the old-fashioned ones, not the electronic, interactive specimens that could walk, groan, eat synthetic honey and hibernate in winter. She also had an impressive collection of glossy books and magazines about bears; she was member of several teddy bear groups, in real life and online, and had even nicknamed her own son 'Teddy'.

We are all passionate about something and Aurelia concluded that Wendy's was a harmless hobby. Cute, even. Besides, don't we all revert to childhood in our old age? If anything, she thought Wendy seemed a little naïve for someone her age, but she was charming, generous and an excellent cook, always happy to share her recipes with Aurelia who, at age 61, was a novice in the kitchen.

Like her bears, Wendy was easy to love, and was indeed much loved by her family, friends and by her husband Peter. Among the plethora of people who often came to visit Wendy, Aurelia had met her sister, her nephew, her nephew's children, and her best friend, Adrianne. She was yet to meet Wendy's son, Teddy, whom she estimated would be in his twenties by now, since Wendy and Peter had been together for 25 years.

'Did you celebrate your silver wedding anniversary?' Aurelia had asked, when Wendy mentioned the length of their union.

'Actually,' Wendy had whispered, as if confessing a secret, 'we are not married. I never got around to divorcing my first husband, so technically, Peter is still my lover.'

And indeed, she called him her 'lover', and he behaved accordingly, serving her breakfast in bed on the weekends, bringing her flowers every Friday, and every now and then, a new bear for her prize-winning collection. Knowing that Aurelia was on her own, he would often lean over her fence on Fridays and offer her a stem of the oriental lilies or irises he bought for Wendy, and he complimented her on her roses.

'Your name should've been Aurelia Green Fingers,

instead of Aurelia Sorrento!' he would say every time. Aurelia, blushing, would cut one of her beautiful roses and give it to him, for Wendy.

During these exchanges, Aurelia had often been tempted to tell Peter her name wasn't really Aurelia Sorrento, but Susan Grey. Aurelia Sorrento had been 'invented' by her manager, Archibald Cornwell, who 35 years ago had decided that with a name like Susan Grey she would never succeed in the world of opera, no matter how talented she was. Unearthing her Italian ancestry, many generations removed, he came up with the theatrical name of Aurelia Sorrento. Multiculturalism was a good thing at that time, and he thought a little foreign flavour would help her public persona. She had become world renowned by this name, particularly after her performance of Rumero's 'Kinship Murmurs' at the closing ceremony of the 2026 Winter Olympic Games in Italy.

One of these days, she thought, she'd tell Peter and Wendy her real name, particularly now she'd decided to lead a new, quiet life as Susan Grey. Not that it mattered, really; a name is just a name, and it wasn't as if she was hiding an earth-shattering secret.

Thinking about her name always brought memories of Archibald, her best friend and manager, the creator of her operatic identity and most of her success, who had died last year at the young age of 62. Aurelia still couldn't believe that at a time when humans had found the cure for diabetes, a vaccine against cancer, had perfected artificial organs and could even bring people back from the dead, provided it was within the hour, Archibald had been instantly killed. He was struck by lightning while playing ball with his grandchild at an otherwise deserted park. By the time the terrified child found his way home alone and help was called, Archibald was too far gone.

His tragic death had made Aurelia reflect upon her own existence, and had made her think about quitting the frantic lifestyle she'd been leading for over three decades: the tours, the planes, the hotels, the concerts, the rehearsals and the teaching. But it had been the headlines in the papers, the day after Archibald's funeral, which had hastened her decision. Photos of her sobbing behind a black veil had been published under the headline 'Diva outmourns widow of dead manager', suggesting in less than subtle words that their relationship hadn't been strictly professional. After all, it had lasted longer than any of Archibald's three marriages.

After this, she decided she had had enough. The month of her sixtieth birthday, not long after Archibald's death, she announced her retirement, found and bought a lovely cottage, and took up gardening.

Peter and Wendy were surprised to find out that until eight months ago Aurelia had never had a garden, given her gift for growing roses, of which she had 11 varieties. There was a rose garden in the cottage when she bought it, but it had been rather lacklustre before she arrived.

Before she retired, she had never owned even a pot plant, because she travelled so far and so often that she couldn't care for anything living, whether plants, pets or children. She had the garden now, and was considering getting a cat, but it was obviously too late for the children. Thankfully, she'd never wanted them so the choice had been easy for her when she had to make it, decades ago, despite the incredible amount of social and family pressure that women like her had to face in the early 2000s.

She had made her decision at a time when, even though the statistics showed that 20 per cent of women in their childbearing years would choose not to have children, those women were still often frowned upon by society. As the years passed, and the figure more than doubled, it became much less of an issue; that's why Aurelia was quite dumbfounded by a comment Wendy made one Friday afternoon as they were sipping tea on Wendy's verandah, waiting for Peter to come home.

'When am I going to meet your children, Rosie?' Wendy had asked, assuming, like so many people did, that Aurelia had grown-up children who had left home long ago. She had a habit of finding nicknames for everybody, and had started to call Aurelia 'Rosie', because of the roses. Aurelia was in fact surprised that Wendy called Peter by his name – when she didn't call him 'lover'.

'I'm afraid you'll never meet them, Wendy. I never had any. I was one of those women who chose career over a family,' Aurelia answered nonchalantly, helping herself to one of Wendy's delicious almond biscuits.

'And to think there are women who would do anything in this world to have a child!' Wendy said, with a deep, melancholic sigh.

Aurelia was startled for a few seconds, remembering how many times she had heard that response in the past, as if one thing had anything to do with the other. When she was 20 years old, she had made a choice between being a ballerina and an opera singer. Nobody had said at the time, 'and to think there are people out there who would do anything to be able to walk, let alone dance.'

And yet, when it came to babies, it was a different matter. In any case, that had been a long time ago, and she hadn't expected to hear it now, in the 2030s, from someone she considered a good friend. She opened her mouth, ready to fire, but realised she couldn't be cross with Wendy.

'I'm sorry about what I said,' Wendy spoke first. 'To cut a long story short, suffice it to say that Teddy is adopted.'

The big, dark-haired former diva and the small ginger-haired lady sat in silence for a while, sipping their tea, the unspoken questions that Aurelia was afraid to utter, hovering between them.

'But you know,' Wendy went on, more animated now, 'Teddy was undoubtedly the second-best thing that happened to me, after Peter. I will never regret rescuing him from who knows what kind of a life he would have had, had we not adopted him.'

'I'd really like to meet Teddy,' Aurelia ventured.

'Well, it's about time you do,' Wendy said, almost back to her usual chirpy self. 'I'll tell you what: come for afternoon tea on Sunday, and I'll introduce you to Teddy. And while you're here, I'll show you my collection of bears. It has won prizes, you know?'

Even though Aurelia had been to their house many times, Wendy had never showed her the bulk of her prize-winning collection, which she kept inside what Aurelia gathered would have been Teddy's old room. This was easy to gather, given that there was a sign on the door reading 'Teddy's room.'

To lighten the mood, they began talking about teddy bears. Wendy explained they'd only been around since the early twentieth century, and owed their name to Theodore (Teddy) Roosevelt, who had refused to shoot a bear during a hunting expedition in 1902. A cartoon of the incident had appeared the next day in the papers, and soon toymakers were selling bears named 'Teddy's Bear', with unparalleled success.

Wendy told Aurelia about the different types of materials and stuffing used to make traditional teddy bears, and from that subject they drifted into the topic of the electronic animal replicas that had been around for years, mostly of domestic animals, and how lifelike they had become.

Without meaning to, they returned to the original subject, of women – or couples – who had chosen not to have children and opted to have pets instead, and later on, due to the demands of their careers and lifestyle choices, they had begun to keep electronic pets instead of real ones. The lifelike robotic pets, which appeared in the early 2010s, had originally been produced as toys for children, or companions to the elderly or the sick. To the amazement of their creators, as they became more sophisticated, they proved to be extremely popular among childless professional couples.

'Even I was thinking, at one point, about getting one of those Hobbocats,' Aurelia confessed, referring to the popular model that, despite a permanent grumpy look on its face, was frighteningly lifelike in every other way. 'But I decided it would be too bizarre. Now that I've retired, I think I'll get a flesh-and-blood one.'

'This reminds me of a book I read as a teenager, written long before I was born.' Wendy smiled sadly. 'By Phillip K. Dick. It was called *Do androids dream of electric sheep?*'

'Wasn't that old movie *Blade Runner* based on that book?' Aurelia said, and Wendy nodded. 'People owned electronic replicas of animals because real animals had become almost extinct. You couldn't tell the difference.'

'It's all happening now, isn't it?' Wendy said. 'Not because animals are extinct but because they've become inconvenient. If the genetic revolutionist movement had had its way, the same would have happened to humans, just like in *Blade Runner*.'

Then Peter arrived with his usual bunch of flowers, disturbing their conversation, and the women parted until the weekend.

Aurelia was indeed impressed by Wendy's collection when she finally saw it on Sunday. No wonder she had been asked to exhibit it many times and had won prizes and praise. There was everything from fully dressed miniature bears no bigger than her thumb, to a real-size, faithful replica of a panda cub, which 'Technically, wasn't a Teddy bear, but is adorable', said Wendy.

There were dozens of bears, sitting on shelves, on cushions, on the floor, on chairs and window sills. Many of them were dressed in costumes: a 19th-century lady, a doctor, a pilot, a nurse, a Santa bear, a king bear, graduate bear, baby bear, and a grandpa bear.

And then, pointing towards a small, tatty bear sitting on top of the bed, she said: 'And that one is my beloved Teddy, our little ray of light.'

For a moment Aurelia thought she'd forgotten how to breathe. Trying to hide her bewilderment she leaned towards Teddy to give him a closer look. It wasn't even an elegant or remarkable bear in any way. This bear was very ordinary, clearly old and rather flaccid, sitting there devoid of a costume or personality. All he had was a bright red ribbon around his neck. Aurelia turned towards Wendy and tried to smile.

'I know what you're thinking,' Wendy said. Aurelia was speechless, so Wendy went on, 'You're thinking that I'm a raving lunatic.'

'Oh, no, not at all…' Aurelia lied.

'Well, many years ago, you would have been dead right.' Wendy said. 'But not now.'

Aurelia lifted her dark eyebrows, as Wendy grabbed her hand and led her outside.

'Let's have our tea,' Wendy said. 'And I'll tell you a story.'

Aurelia heard that when Wendy was still married, over 30 years ago, she'd had a nervous breakdown following a miscarriage that resulted in her not being able to have children. After her breakdown, her marriage collapsed, she lost her job and for a while, she was indeed behaving like a 'raving lunatic' until her best friend, Adrianne, took her to see a doctor. She'd met Peter soon after, through a support group.

'Peter and I became the best of friends, but our relationship wasn't going anywhere,' Wendy said, looking into the distance as if contemplating the past. 'I was 40 years old and wanted to settle down, but we'd become stuck. One day I went furniture shopping with Adrianne, and we saw this little bear sitting on top of a leather couch. Addie bought the couch, together with thousands of dollars' worth of furniture. I had bought nothing. So, Addie urged me to buy at least the bear. She couldn't let me go home empty handed and without having spent a cent, when she had spent a fortune! I wasn't into teddy bears at that point...

'"Oh my God!" Peter exclaimed that night, when he came to visit me and saw the bear, sitting on my sofa. He took it in his arms and cuddled it. "This looks just like the first bear I ever had," he told me. "I treasured that bear, but it got mysteriously lost during a move when I was about ten." He said he suspected his mother "lost" it, worried that he was too old to play with stuffed toys.

"What's his name?" he asked me and I replied, '"Teddy!" as I was unable to come up with anything more original.'

Wendy paused, refilling Aurelia's cup and checking she was still breathing. Not only was she breathing, but she was also eager to know more.

'And?' Aurelia asked.

'As crazy as it sounds, Rosie, Teddy changed the course of our relationship, and our life. We started treating him as our child, the child we never had. Peter had been married before, and his wife had not wanted children.'

After Teddy, Wendy explained, came the other bears, mostly bought by Peter. She made the costumes.

'But none of them can take Teddy's place in my heart.' At this, she went inside and came back carrying Teddy. 'He has personality!'

In her dexterous hands, Teddy suddenly became alive: he tilted his head to the side and looked at Aurelia intently, and then frowned – with a little help from her fingers – before turning around to look at his owner, nodding his head in approval.

'He likes you,' Wendy said, her eyes brightening. Because he wasn't a rigid bear, he could be manipulated like a puppet. Aurelia realised she'd never asked Wendy what her occupation had been. She wondered if she had been a professional puppeteer.

'And since today is secret-sharing day,' Wendy said later, when she was walking Aurelia to the front gate. 'You might as well know that Peter's real name isn't Peter; it's Gordon. I nicknamed him Peter after Peter Pan. You know, Peter Pan and Wendy.'

'Speaking of real names,' Aurelia said, just before she walked out of the gate. 'You might as well know my name is not real either. It's not Aurelia, and my surname is not Sorrento. I'm Susan Grey.'

And then she walked away, leaving Wendy with a puzzled look on her face.

As Aurelia was removing her makeup that night, she felt a pang of sorrow for Wendy, which extended to Peter-Gordon. How sad it was that their little ray of light was a stuffed bear, even if they were perfectly aware of how strange that was. But then she looked at herself in the mirror for a while, and her whole glitzy life paraded in front of her, culminating at the point she was at tonight. All alone, with nothing but a rose garden and the memory of long-gone achievements to keep her going. She realised that of the two of them, Wendy was certainly not the maddest, nor the saddest.

And Susan Grey decided that instead of a cat, she would get a teddy bear, and name him Archie. He would have plenty of friends, and at least she knew he would never die or leave her.

Encounter in the Bush

Carly, Bea and Trish set off early on a Saturday morning for their monthly bushwalk. It had been nearly a year since they'd started the walking group and gradually, they had become more adventurous. First, there had been beach strolls, bay walks and park runs, mostly on the North Shore, where they lived. Two hours at the most, always followed by lunch at a local cafe. Then they ventured out into reserves, some of which were many kilometres away from home, and finally, into the proper bush, where there were no cafes to be found.

They had never been the type of women who would go windsailing, bungee jumping, mountain climbing or parachuting. Those were activities their teenage children did, and occasionally, their husbands. Once upon a time, in their university days, they had all belonged to a netball team. That had been over 20 years ago, before work, marriage and families, before they gave birth to a total of seven children between them.

But walking was something they could all handle: one foot in front of the other, one step at a time. Carly, in particular, had grown up in the highlands of the Andes and felt much more comfortable hiking than swimming. In fact, the eucalyptus trees reminded her vividly of her childhood. It was one of the few plant species that thrived at high altitude and gum trees populated the streets and the bush in her hometown, so she felt right at home in the Australian wilderness.

With time, their steps became firmer, longer and steeper. Soon they purchased equipment: daypacks, hiking shoes, walking poles, water bladders, a compass. They were proud to give the impression they were professional bushwalkers.

This particular track was the hardest they would be attempting in the year since they started walking. It would cover 19 kilometres, take seven hours and included creek crossings, steep, forested slopes, deep valleys and a waterfall. It had been Carly's turn to choose the walk, and she picked this one out of a book. The description said the navigation was tricky, so they had their compass with them, although they were never sure if they were using it correctly. She had cooked Saturday's dinner the previous night as she expected to be exhausted by the time she arrived home. She kissed her husband goodbye, but he didn't take any notice. He was still asleep when she left.

The walk was harder than they had anticipated. The terrain was rough and undulating, there was more climbing than they thought there would be, the creek crossings were tricky, and at times the track all but disappeared amidst fallen trees and dense bushes. Trish tripped twice on the fallen tree branches, and Bea's water bladder leaked inside her bag, soaking her mobile phone. Still, they were rewarded with magnificent views of the waterfall, the river and the valley; the wild spring flowers were in full bloom, it was perfect weather, and they enjoyed a pleasant picnic lunch by the river.

After six hours of walking on uneven terrain, fatigue began to set in. When they came upon yet another creek, where water trickled over slippery boulders covered with moss, they decided to take their time, and they carefully negotiated their way across, one by one. Just then, they were overtaken by a young man, who appeared out of nowhere, wearing nothing but a pair of hot pink shorts. Barefoot, he breezed past the three women who were struggling and scrambling their way, using feet, poles and hands.

Carly, who was last in the file, couldn't believe it. How could anyone walk that rough, slippery track barefoot, and with such ease? As she was thinking this, she skidded and landed on her backside, her leg sliding between two boulders. Searing pain shot up her shin, but her friends, who were walking ahead, didn't see her fall and kept clambering their way across the creek.

Carly was about to call out to them when she realised the young man had suddenly materialised next to her. He must have heard her weak yelp, and had come back. He had his arm stretched out.

'You okay?' he said. He had green eyes, tanned skin, toned muscles and blond hair down to his shoulders. 'Can I give you a hand?'

'I-I'm okay, I think,' Carly managed to say. 'I c-c-could do with a hand, thanks!'

The man deftly helped her up to her feet, picked up her walking pole with one hand, and supported her weight by gripping her elbow, walking by her side until they made it safely across to the other side of the creek. By then, Trish and Bea had realised what happened and were gesturing and shouting their concern.

'You gonna be okay walking from here?' he said before he deposited her safely into the hands of her friends.

'I-I should be,' Carly stuttered again. Her legs were shaking, but not from the fall. 'It's sore, but I don't think anything is broken. Thanks so much, you are a lifesaver!'

'It's nothing – I grew up around here, so I know this track like the back of my hand,' he said. 'It can be tricky in some parts.'

'You are obviously a very well brought-up young man,' Bea said.

'Yeah, I doubt my son would be so kind!' added Trish. 'Not that I didn't bring him up well...'

'See you later, then,' the man said to the women and was on his way. Just before he disappeared among the bushes, Carly caught a glimpse of his smiling face, and she could have sworn he winked at her.

When they got over the excitement and made sure Carly wasn't seriously injured, the women resumed their hike, slowing right down to allow for Carly's hobbling. They still had another three kilometres to go.

But Carly wasn't thinking about her leg, or about the dull pangs of pain that shot up her shin with every step, or how she would not have been able to get out if she didn't have her trusty walking pole to lean on. She kept thinking of the young man, whom she baptised Todd.

She thought of Todd's perfect teeth, his long blond hair, his naked chest, the way he firmly held her hand and lifted her up like a feather, his parting wink. It had been years since anyone other than her husband had winked at her, or flirted with her, or touched her, and even her husband didn't do much of that anymore – after all, they had been married for over two decades.

She imagined what would have happened if Trish and Bea hadn't been around. She imagined Todd examining the scratches on her leg, feeling her shin and her calves to make sure they were okay.

'Just a minor scratch on your shin... but what a nice calf! You must be a professional bushwalker,' he was saying, before his hand slid further up her shorts. She imagined him lifting her in his arms and carrying her into the wilderness—

'... your son's age,' she heard Bea say.

'Sorry, what did you say? I was miles away,' Carly said, reluctantly returning from fantasy land. Bea was walking next to her; the path had evened up and they were very close to the end.

'That nice boy, he must have been about your son's age.'

'Do you really think so? I would've thought he was much older!'

'No, he was Jamie's age, give or take a couple of years.'

'Ugh!' Carly said, feeling a shiver from head to toe.

'What's wrong? Is your leg hurting?' said Trish.

'Nothing. Nothing is wrong. Are we nearly there? I've had enough!' said Carly, expelling all thoughts of Todd out of her mind. A purple bruise was quickly spreading over her shin. 'Whose idea was it to do this damn hard walk, anyway?'

愖

The young man, whose real name was Bruce, found his friends by the riverbed, not far from the creek. They had been canoeing all day and were eager to get back into the water one last time before the sun set.

'Where were you, man? How far did you have to go to take a piss?'

'I got sidetracked. I ran into these old ducks, and one of them fell on her arse just as I was walking past. What could I do? I had to help her up!'

'Well, old ducks should know better than to walk on this track – it's not meant for wimps.'

'Yeah, but you should have seen how they fussed and carried on. They even said I was well brought up!'

The group exploded in laughter. 'Well brought up! Now that's the funniest thing we've heard in a long time!' said one of them.

With that, they pushed their canoes into the water and rowed away.

The Messenger

A white creature is floating above him. At first, he thinks it is a pigeon, but then he realises it is just a plastic bag swaying in the draught, merging with the shadows and reappearing in the weak moonlight that seeps through a hole in the ceiling – some sort of crude skylight.

He is in a room that is empty but for his presence and the chair he has been sitting in for some days now – how many he can't tell or remember. His hands are tied behind the chair. During the day, the warmth of the sun makes his situation more bearable, but it is night-time now, and it's freezing. The only thing that gives him some comfort is the moon, curled up as if smiling, as if telling him not to give up.

He looks up again, despite the pain in his neck and shoulders, and sees that the plastic bag is still dancing in the air just above him. He closes his eyes, and when he opens them, he finds himself in a park. His clothes are clean and his body is not bruised or broken. It is warm and sunny, and he is surrounded by flower beds and trees. Hovering over him is not a plastic bag but a pigeon.

He reaches out with his palm up, and the bird obediently sits on it. He notices it is carrying a little tube, tied to its foot. He opens the tube to find a handwritten message.

'Don't give up,' it says.

He wakes up, realising he has passed out from exhaustion, or is hallucinating due to hunger, thirst and concussion. It is dark again and his broken body reeks of blood, sweat and other bodily fluids.

He notices the plastic bag is now static, lying on the floor not far from him; he can barely make out its shape. Suddenly he remembers that at one point, one of his tormentors had put the plastic bag over his head, threatening to suffocate him. He must have left it behind.

He remembers his father's warnings about the dangers of political activism. Circumstances were particularly volatile under the current dictatorship, and thousands of militants – and also innocent people who had nothing to do with anything – had already 'disappeared'. However, he is sure his father wouldn't be recriminating him now, saying 'I told you so'. Instead, he would be telling him not to give up.

He hears voices outside the door and a shiver runs up his spine. Making an effort to control his panic, he closes his eyes and pretends to be unconscious. Two men come in, their faces hidden underneath balaclavas.

'What's that on the floor?' one of them says.

'It must be something we dropped,' the other one says, kicking the plastic bag away and picking up a scrunched-up piece of paper. 'It's a note.'

'What does it say?' the first one says.

'Don't give up,' reads the second one.

'Don't give up?' the first man says, grabbing his victim by the hair, forcing him to lift his head.

'I'll teach him not to give up!'

He feels the full force of the blow on his face, but there is no pain. Another blow follows on the torso, but his chest is also anaesthetised. He keeps his eyes tightly shut, and when he finally opens them, he is no longer in the room.

He is walking on the moon, feeling light as a feather and free at last. From up there he can just make out, through the skylight far below, two figures brutally bashing what seems to be a lifeless rag doll.

PART 3:
BIRTH OF AN ANGEL
FIVE INTERTWINED STORIES

I. Origins

I will not mention his name, for he is still walking the pathways of some faraway place, shaking warm sand from his bare feet; because his voice is still resounding in my ears, or perhaps because he no longer has a name. Neither will I give him a fictitious name. You give fictitious names to those who have never existed, or to legends that nobody truly believes.

I am not fictitious either. We both exist and are still dancing like leaves in the wind, although not with each other. I know he exists, because for many nights he slept in my bed, because I gave birth to his children, who were born wide-eyed and aware, with a smile on their faces, already glad to be alive.

We are both real; perhaps everything else is fiction. A mixture of fantasies and memories, and most of all, of dreams: his dreams. The dreams that remained unfinished when he woke up screaming, covered in sweat and shuddering with fever, in the middle of the night... night after night.

Until one day, weary and sleepless (for he started to be afraid of sleep), he decided to go out into the world to search for the voice that had not yet called him. He could no longer wait in this limbo, where he was neither ordinary man nor prophet. This waiting was like a continuous state of flux, a death of a kind; or more precisely, a never-ending birth.

In the meantime, I blossomed, in the autumn of my life. After so many years, I finally came to terms with the fact that his happiness – or mine – did not depend upon the other, but it was up to each of us to find our own. I let him go without tears; something unusual for me. But not before I made sure I kept the secret treasure of the two hearts that were beating inside my womb and the priceless gift he left inside my mind: his dreams.

It is in the realm of the dreams that he visits and re-visits me, realising himself one and a thousand times, in one and a thousand ways. These are the dreams that I now cast into the world, in the same way that one day I will cast his ashes to the wind, as he requested. Because I know that sooner or later, he will come back, even if it is only to bid me farewell.

Thus, I dry my tears and discover that my eyes are bright like my children's, and when I open them to see life in this new light, it is just in time to witness, at last, the final phase of his transformation.

2. The Reluctant Prophet

I was walking on the beach on a fine autumn afternoon. It was full of people; many of them children. They were watching some kind of spectacle; a stage had been set up on the sand, with the sea in the background. When I arrived, there was a musical group on the stage, dressed in colourful ponchos and sombreros.

My ears were overwhelmed by the sound of strings, percussion and pan flutes intermingled with the crashing of waves and the murmurs of the crowd. The audience had their arms raised, swaying from one side to the other, to the rhythm of the music, the breeze ruffling their hair. Everyone seemed in a celebratory mood, although many of the children were clearly unwell.

Away from the group there was a child dressed in humble clothes. He was also entranced by the music but there was no joy in his eyes. There was, however, an aura emanating from him that I recognised. I approached him, yet before I could say a word he started speaking. The voice that came out of his throat, deep and grave, was unbecoming for a child his age.

'When you have children, take good care of them,' he

said. 'Lest they end up like me. In this world, my only family is myself. I will always be a misfit.'

'Who are you, child, to judge and condemn yourself so harshly, and speak with such hopelessness?' I replied. 'You don't even know yourself, and have no idea of what you can become. And I tell you now: you are greater than all of them – I gestured towards the crowd – and any of us, for not only do you have the gift of healing, but you are also a prophet.'

The child looked at me with mistrust in his eyes. The kind of bitterness you only see in old people, who on the verge of death know it is too late to do anything with their lives. He got up and began to walk away from me, shaking his head, as if he had just heard the words of a lunatic. I went after him, determined to be heard. Pointing at him with my index finger, I started repeating: 'A healer and a prophet... A healer and a prophet!'

At the rhythm of my words, which were becoming louder and louder, the astonished child was wrapped in a whirlpool of wind, sand and water, which ripped apart his clothes, leaving him naked at first and then, dressed only in a white tunic, with a turban on his head.

Even then, he did not surrender. Refusing to believe his senses, he still tried to get away, yelling incomprehensibly. But as he made his way through the crowd, some of the sick children in his path started screaming with joy. A girl who could only see with one eye, felt the sightless eye suddenly swamped by a blinding light, and then a full, clear vision of the blue sky. A boy who had a skin condition that covered his arms with hideous sores, saw his wounds close and disappear, leaving a clean, smooth skin.

At this, the musicians stopped playing, and everybody turned around in complete silence to look at the child. Flushing with anger and shame, all he wanted to do was disappear.

'Look at me,' he managed to say. 'I look ridiculous in this … attire.'

'You can't deny your destiny,' I said. 'For even if you don't do it willingly, your shadow will heal wherever you go. Behold! A healer and a prophet,' I started my mantra again. 'A healer and a prophet!'

And I repeated the five words incessantly, my voice becoming louder and stronger every time, to the great bewilderment of the child dressed in white. When I turned towards the crowd, expecting them to throw stones at me, assuming me demented, I was astonished to hear their voices joining mine. The parents, the children, even the musicians with their drums, formed a chorus whose voices pulsated above the sound of the waves. 'A healer and a prophet! A healer and…'

Finally, those eyes that only minutes ago had glared with hostility and – I suspected – had never cried before, filled with tears, and the child came towards me.

'Master,' he said, trembling, moved by the clamour of voices he could hear not only outside, but also within. 'Master, you win, I will do as you say, but… what exactly is a *prophet*?'

3. The Window

I have always been a monster. Today I stand in threadbare clothes in the semi-darkness of my room, in front of a full-size mirror. Outside, the town is waking up to a new dawn, unaware of my existence. I have not ventured beyond these walls for many years, but today I have decided it is time for everyone to see me, in all my deformity. I will not spare them the sight any longer. It is time for me to end the misery, the solitude I call life.

The mirror is covered with a black cloth. My hand trembles as I reach for the cloth, which I placed there when I was first moved into this room. I have never wanted to look at my reflection; I don't know the colour of my eyes, the appearance of my features, the shape of this body that has caused me so much pain. But I gather all my strength, for I will need it to do what I must do.

The 13 years of my life run through my mind in that moment of hesitation. Not all my memories are bleak. I was a light-hearted child when I lived with my mother in the forest.

⋘

My mother told me that she was very young, almost a child when she had me. She didn't even know she was pregnant. When she started to grow bigger, she thought she was gaining weight, retaining water. Maybe that was also part of all the other changes that overcame her body when she reached the age of 13.

There was nobody to tell her otherwise. Her own mother died when she was born; being a very old woman she could not survive childbearing. My mother grew up with her elderly father and had made nothing of her swelling stomach and the discomfort until she felt the pain. My grandfather assisted her with the labour. She said that as soon as she held me in her arms, she started to cry... and cry she would, for years to come.

She cried because her baby girl was not a regular child; she had two enormous humps on her tiny back.

As I grew up, they looked like breasts, except they were not fleshy, but hard - and they were on the wrong side of my body. They seemed to grow bigger every year.

The people in the town used to throw stones and curses at my mother when she went out. Not only had she conceived without a man, but she had given birth to a monster. I could only be the incarnation of evil. So, when my grandfather died, we moved into the forest.

But when I was seven years old, I killed my mother.

ଔ

Her eyes were the same colour as the leaves of the peppercorn tree in spring. Her hair, a dark golden shade, was long and silky. She used to sing for me while she brushed my hair. She never cut it because it was even more beautiful than hers, and it covered the humps on my back.

My mother would rub my back every night with an unguent made of rare leaves, lavender petals and sunflower oil, with the conviction that this concoction would magically stop the bony lumps on my back from growing.

'Three is a number of wonder and miracles,' she would say. 'The trinity.' And every night, when she did this, she would cry, her warm tears mixing with the ointment. I was too young to understand her sadness and I would sing merry songs to stop her weeping.

One morning she went out to fetch the leaves and never came back. I waited in our shack for two, three, maybe five days. I didn't eat, I didn't sleep. I just cried and screamed, calling her name to exhaustion, until I my voice become a silent wail.

Then four strangers came. A woman, a man and two boys, about my age. While I was sitting in a corner of the shack, terrified, the woman told me she was a distant relative of my mother. She said my mother had died and I had to go and live with them. She picked me up, and then let me go with a scream when she felt my humps. 'Lord, she really *is* deformed!'

'Shhh! you will frighten the creature. What is your name, child?' asked the man, parting my long hair so he could see my face, covered with dirt and streaked by the tears.

But I could not answer. Firstly, because my mother never gave me a name. Secondly, even if I had one (I thought of the many names mother called me: sunflower, little angel, child of God... among others) I couldn't find my voice. I had lost it while crying and calling my mother's name, and since then I have not been able to speak again.

The man covered me with a black cloth and carried me to their house in town. They didn't know what to do with me. Not only was I a monster, but also they could not communicate with me. They thought since I could not speak, that I couldn't understand what they said to me either. They set me up in their attic; and this has been my home for the last six years.

I heard them say my mother had slipped and fallen over the side of the mountain trying to get the leaves she used for my unguent. She had broken her neck. But I think what really happened is that she cried herself to death. Either way, it was my fault. I killed my mother; I had begun killing her, slowly, the day I was born.

⚃

I look at the door of my room. Through that door, when it is still dark, servants bring food for me to eat and fresh water so I can wash. Swiftly and silently, they take away all my waste and leave. They never speak to me.

I am not a prisoner here; the door is never locked. I could go down those stairs any day, but I cannot see a reason to do that. To sit at the same table with these relatives who are afraid of me? To walk into the streets, where my mother was insulted and stoned by people who could not accept my difference? Or to escape into the forest again, where I will be as lonely as I am here? No. If there is a way out of here, I know it is not through that door.

There is a pigeon at my window, its head tilted to the side, staring at my humps. Or perhaps it is just looking at me for what I am, a harmless girl? It makes noises, as if it wants to talk to me. I approach it, but it flees. And I wish I could fly with it, free, into the clear sky.

Ↄ

After I turned 13, everything in my body started to grow. My breasts began swelling, hair appeared between my legs and under my arms, and my hated humps also seemed to bulge out of control. Not knowing what to do, I wrapped my chest with a cloth, so tight I could hardly breathe, to stop the lumps from growing, both at the front and at the back. But trapped beneath the cloth, they kept on swelling, I could feel them. Determined to die, I stopped eating my food.

The servants kept bringing a fresh plate of food every day and removing the one that was still full, without saying a word. Maybe my relatives would have been relieved if I died of my own will; maybe that would have solved their problem. I don't know. All I know is that nobody came to ask me to eat. This went on for over a week. I was beginning to feel weak and disoriented, when one night someone came to visit.

At first, I thought I was dreaming. A young man was sitting on my bed, watching me sleep. He removed the covers, and his hand, slipping under my gown, travelled from my knees to my thighs, stopped for a moment between my legs. I felt its warmness up my belly, my ribcage, until it reached my chest. It felt the bandage, and followed it around to my back. It touched my humps, and rested there for some time. I opened my eyes, and he looked back at me. He didn't look away. He didn't run in disgust. I recognised his face; he was one of my cousins; I had seen him, still a boy, that day in the woods. He held my face with both hands, and said:

'Poor, poor creature… and you have the face of an angel.'

I opened my mouth to speak to him, but only a grunt came from my throat. Only then he seemed to wake up from his own dream. He stood up and ran down the stairs. Perhaps he thought I was going to scream.

But I wasn't going to scream… on the contrary, I wanted to ask him to stay, to touch me again, to slip inside my bed and tell me stories about the world outside. To tell me what lay beyond the town, beyond the forest and the mountains. To tell me his name, and what was that sensation I felt when he touched me.

I regained my will to live and began to eat again. Somehow in his eyes, his touch, in what he said to me, I suspected the existence of something other than despair and fear. A sort of tenderness, a kindness I could only recall feeling from my mother. And I waited night after night, with the hope that he would return, but he never did.

ত

I have decided now I can no longer wait for death, I will have to go and find her. I am tired of this life. I have no happiness, no pleasure, no comfort. I know now the only way for me to find relief is through that window. I look outside: down below is the town, still in semi-darkness, the market place, the narrow streets. Above is the sky, and beyond, I can see the misty mountains.

I strip down to my undergarments and slowly wash

my body. I let my hair loose; it has been wrapped around my head for a long time, since I started to step on it when I walked around the room. I wash my face and painstakingly undo the bandage around my chest, and wash my breasts. The weight in my back is almost crushing, I can hardly stand straight.

I stand in front of the mirror; it is time. I must jump out of that window before the servants come. Let all these people who didn't want me to exist, see me lying in the middle of their marketplace, with a broken neck just like my mother.

I am ready to take my life, but I am not sure I am ready to uncover that mirror. Shaking, I pull the black cloth. It falls to the floor.

I look at my reflection in the mirror. My body, slender and pale; my firm breasts; my skin, almost translucent; my eyes, green like my mother's; and my light-golden hair, so light it is almost the colour of snow, flowing down to the floor. And behind me, the two huge things that used to be my humps, have grown and unfurled once I let them free.

Suddenly, I realise I am not a monster.

I am beautiful, beautiful beyond belief. Yet my beauty is above what the people of this house, the inhabitants of this town can comprehend. I am not like them; this is not my place. I don't belong here. Or perhaps I do, but they are not ready for me.

I walk towards the window; instinctively, I know what to do. I know the only way to freedom is through that window. I climb onto the sill and stand on the cornice for a few moments. Below, some people are already moving; a woman has seen me and has started to yell. They are gathering, screaming, flapping their arms. I feel the cold breeze of the morning caressing my naked skin.

I take one last look at my room, at the humid walls, the dusty floor, the stained sheets of my bed, the lonely mirror. Perhaps one day I will return... but not in this life.

I look again at the sky, the sun rising over the mountains. Perhaps there I will find others like me. The sky, the sky, that is where I belong. So I take a deep breath, spread my magnificent, white feathered wings...

... and jump.

4. The Day the Master Fell

*P**erfundus: 'He who inspires, who endows, who heals, who purifies.'*[1]

I have the certainty that I existed before this life, a long, long time ago.

So long ago that my own memories fade in the mists of time. But a part of who I was is still fresh, still alive within me, and carries a darkness that is real and palpable, infinite. A darkness that has been with me for centuries. That is how I know I existed, the same way I exist today, within this ephemeral body with a mind bestowed with only inconsequential powers. But I know I was once unique, powerful, virtually infinite and almost immortal.

I was a Master.

ಳ

Earth was very different in those days. Since then, new continents have appeared from nowhere, others have

---

1 From the Latin ***Perfundo***: (a) to soak, wet, flood, dye; (b) to besprinkle, bathe, anoint; (c) to bestrew, scatter over; (d) to inspire, fill, imbue – *Langenscheidt Latin-English Dictionary*

shifted or have been reclaimed by the oceans. There were mountains that do not exist today and the seas covered lands that are now verdant. There were jungles and exuberant rainforests where we can now see only deserts. Some of those changes were natural, but others were the product of the ignorance or wickedness of people. Some were catastrophic and inevitable: earthquakes, tidal waves, the earth protesting against the multiple assaults to which she is subjected by humankind.

Some of these changes, though, were the feats of beings such as the one I used to be. We could alter the course of rivers, move mountains, change the shape of canyons and peninsulas, control wind, storm and fire. Gods? No, gods never inhabited the earth. Somewhere in the universe, wherever they dwell, they might be vaguely aware of this planet's existence, but they have never lived here.

We were often mistaken for gods. There were a few of us scattered throughout the planet, but we rarely came across each other.

I had the ability to choose whom I wanted to be, my appearance and faculties. And I made myself powerful and mighty, so no-one could harm me.

I had been a mortal child once and had seen enough destruction around me. In the village of straw-roofed huts where I lived with my family, we often saw death and trag-edy. Time and again we witnessed the barbarians coming to ransack our homes, set the villages on fire, rape the women, slaughter the men and kidnap the children.

One night I woke up to find myself restrained by the neck, like a dog. The dying fires outside emanated enough flickering light to allow me to witness my parents being slaughtered in front of my eyes, drowning in their own blood while I could do nothing to help them. That was the last time I cried, my tears mixing with the acrid taste of my own bile.

And I swore that I would never, ever again be a feeble being, subjected to such outrage, pain and anguish. I became insensitive and bitter, and wandered the streets looking after no-one but myself. Until one day, still a child, I met a Master, who singled me out in a crowd. He said I was a healer and a prophet, and had special powers. He said he could show me how to use them. Reluctantly, I followed him, but soon afterwards he too abandoned me – perhaps his presence was required elsewhere. It did not matter, for he had shown me all I needed to know. Without him, I grew without limits, controllers or opponents, until my power was immeasurable.

I could alter the shape of both living and inert entities; I could change the weather and the seasons at my will. I could play with the destinies of mortals and destroy those whom I judged harmful or unfair. The barbarians never came across my path again. However, I did not go after them, because vengeance would have been a waste of my energy; I knew they would end up slaughtering one another – and so they did.

But power tastes like a sweet and extraordinary elixir that intoxicates and blinds. This heavenly nectar overwhelmed my senses and my mind. I lost my foresight, my compassion and my sensibility.

And one day, I killed an innocent being.

☙

My doom came upon me one early spring morning, when it was still cold. In the middle of an endless wasteland with nothing except sand for over one hundred miles around, a huge rock appeared from nowhere. It was not my doing; this was my desert and I had not changed it.

I had never come across such a phenomenon before. As I drew closer, I noticed a small, famished-looking creature, almost naked, covered only by a white tunic. So minute, so fragile she was, with her pale skin almost stuck to her bones. She resembled a crystalline insect, hardly visible against the immensity of the desert. Sitting on the rock, she seemed to be meditating. Or perhaps she had been there, patiently waiting for me, since the beginning of time?

Her features resembled a child's, yet it was impossible to know her age because her transparent eyes exuded the sort of wisdom that can only be accumulated through centuries of experience. Her hair was so light in colour and weight that it floated behind her like a hazy mass of white feathers.

My first impulse was to make her disappear, with the simple snap of my fingers. But I could not, because I was instantly entranced by her translucent gaze. I observed she was not sitting on the rock, but levitating above it. Her voice was soft and musical, like the chant of the birds that I once heard when I was a child, in another life.

'Perfundus,' she said, shaking her head, 'Look what you have become. You want to annihilate an innocent being just because you cannot accept that something can occur outside your control.'

I opened my mouth in rage to admonish the creature, yet no words found their way to my tongue. I had killed many mortals, that was true. But they were all criminals, imbeciles. This creature was not like them; but the impulse of destruction blinded me. Unperturbed, she went on speaking.

'You have become this way because you are afraid,' she said, a subtle smile in her colourless lips. 'Afraid of falling, of being hurt, of being vulnerable and making mistakes. Afraid of being human. That is why you became powerful beyond measure. Invulnerable, inhuman. You, who call yourself "The Master", have absolute control over your domain and everything that comes near it. But in the end, you have the soul of a child, because you are afraid.'

I could not accept such words. To see this minute being, who spoke so softly I could barely hear her, talking to me in that manner! To me, who could make her disappear in the blink of an eye if I wanted to! She was doomed.

'No,' she said, holding one hand in front of her. 'You cannot destroy me until I have said what I came here to say.' At these words, I felt every muscle of my body go numb. I was paralysed. 'With the power that you have, you can change the course of history, and yet you do not know the limits of your blindness. With that same power you can cause the destruction of mankind. Your presence on earth is too disturbing; the changes you are creating are not permitted. You are altering the order of life. One man, and yet, so full of himself, that he has forgotten the one quality that gives me life, that nourishes me: *compassion*.'

She paused, letting the word reverberate in my mind for a few moments. I had heard someone say that to me a long time before.

'Be compassionate, child, for you never know what

turns your fate will take'. It had been my mother, not long before she was killed.

'I knew you before you came into being, since you were no more than a caterpillar. I have observed your metamorphosis, and it has been decided that you can no longer follow this course. But I am here to offer you a second chance.'

She stood up, and she seemed to have grown, for now she was almost my height. Slender and tall, and suddenly she radiated impossible beauty, the kind of beauty that can be blinding. 'I am The Enlightened.' she said. 'And I have come to invite you to walk with me and follow the path of compassion. If we join our power – yours, mine and that of The One who sends me, we could make wonders happen on earth.'

She extended her pale arm towards me, but I was still unable to move. I knew what she was doing: she was trying to seduce me into her ways. All she wanted was to win this battle while my physical powers were rendered useless.

'Otherwise, as soon as I have finished uttering these words, you can destroy me,' she said, with sadness. 'It is your choice. But I must warn you: that will mean your own destruction.'

I did not hear her last words. As I regained my power, her last sentence was blurred in an incomprehensible murmur. My vision was blocked by a wrath outside my control. The sweat of rage ran down my forehead, a bitter taste bathed my senses: blood.

How could this threadbare creature tell me what I need, give me choices, show me what path I must follow! I AM THE MASTER, and only I know what I need and where I am going, and there is no-one more powerful than me!

And with one impulse of my will, I annihilated her.

Except that she did not simply disappear, but her body slowly faded in a column of smoke, a sort of essence, that was perfume and music at the same time; it was compassion, truth ... *love*?

What a strange word. '*Love, love...*' Her dimming voice kept echoing inside my head. As the column of smoke ascended to the sky, as if propelled by wings, I noticed that white flowers were growing on the rock where she had been sitting. And I understood. The sudden realisation resounded and bounced against the walls of my skull until my head felt as if it was going to explode.

I understood that I had destroyed the emissary who had wanted to show me the only way there was.

Too late, I understood the meaning of compassion, of love, of those who die to redeem others. She had died for me. She, whom I had killed, *loved* me; from the beginning of time, she'd loved me. And I could no longer exist with that sorrow. It was a weight that crushed my mind and body; and so, closing my eyes, I made my heart stop.

On the ground where my body fell, nothing was left. Not flowers, not essence, nor music, ashes or bones. Only a black shadow, an infinite darkness, where I remained for countless centuries, waiting for the second chance she promised.

5. The Visitor

My wife wasn't home when it arrived. Only my mother and I saw its shadow crawling outside the door, darkening the whole landscape. It were as if night had suddenly fallen upon us, and when I ventured outside, I could barely distinguish its deformed silhouette: the vampire wings, the blood-stained eyes and horrible hooves instead of feet. But above all, the long and pointed black horns.

It was a dense mass of black energy, absorbing all life and light around it. We couldn't see anything beyond its shadow. It was as if it had taken the light and the warmth of the summer afternoon away, because everything went dark and my mother and I started shivering helplessly, shaken by a sudden chill, which we could not tell apart from the horror we felt. Worst of all was the smell. Putrid, pervasive; we had to stop ourselves from breathing until we got used to it. It was an outrageous violation of our senses.

I understood it had come to fetch me. But I didn't know why.

My mother overcame her fear for an instant and managed to find the silver crucifix that she always carried in her bag, and gave it to me, convinced that the very sight of it would scare the malignant being away.

I held it, but more because of what I was taught to believe as a child than for the faith that my mother had in the cross, which was as solid as its silver and as palpable as the terror that filled her in those moments. My faith in such things was at that moment in my life very questionable. Perhaps that was why the creature didn't even blink at the sight of it. Instead, it burst into roaring laughter when I approached the door holding the crucifix with my arms crossed over my chest.

It seemed my weakness was nourishment to it, because the more my faith waned, the more it grew in size. By the time I ran back inside, slamming the door behind me, terrified, with 'my tail tucked between my legs' (as my wife would have said if she were there) and the crucifix barely hanging from my fingers, it had reached the aspect and the proportions of a giant, repulsive, fire-breathing monster.

But then my wife appeared, inside the house. I don't know how she came in, because I was at the door the whole time and never saw her arrive. She seemed more indignant than frightened. She still had in her hands the mail that she'd collected on her way in, and a brown paper bag with croissants for afternoon tea.

It seemed to me she walked straight past our visitor, completely oblivious to its presence, the gloominess and the stench surrounding it. Like the good manager she was, and before I could say anything, she painted me the picture in one single brushstroke:

'And what is your plan now? We have worked so hard and for so many years to pay off this house, and you are going to let *that thing* come right here, into our own home, and threaten us like this?'

'We could push the desk against the door so it can't get in...?'

'What?' she said, incredulous. She took a moment to calm down, and then she said: 'Do you remember, years ago, when you used to tell me that I should be more asser-tive, that I should have more faith in myself? Don't you think your advice worked wonders? Look at me now! Well, Mister, now you have to apply the same principles to yourself!'

I was staring at her, speechless. 'Go on, do something!' she went on. 'Look, everything is so dark on the verandah, all my plants will die!'

She gave me a slight push towards the door, and shut herself in the bedroom with my mother – but not before switching on the kettle for afternoon tea. As she closed the door, I thought I heard her mutter the word 'wimp'.

That was what did the trick. I was more agitated by that word than by the presence of evil incarnate on my porch. She was right: I had to do something.

A sudden clarity took over my mind at that moment. I realised the monster brought the dark with it because it hated the light. I snapped my fingers, opened the door and switched on the big light on the porch.

When I did this, something strange happened: as soon as I turned it on, the little globe in our porch emanated a light that was more powerful than anything I could imag-ine; it was as bright as the sun. I had to move backwards, covering my eyes until I got used to it.

Bewildered, the monster jumped back, growling, the red eyes flickering with fire.

'Aha!' I said, a growing feeling of confidence taking over my entire body and mind. 'You don't like the light, do you? Well, from now on, day and night, there will always be a light outside this house.' As I said this, I was amazed at the sound of my own voice, which was deeper and stronger than ever before.

It was then the phenomenon started. In the darkness of the sky, I could perceive dense clouds travelling at a surprising speed, gathering, appearing from nowhere. I called my wife. Without much enthusiasm, she came out. My mother stayed in the room.

'Look!' I said to her. 'You never believe me when I tell you that before some things happen, I already know them... Or when we see a movie and I can foresee the ending, but because I always keep it to myself you never believe me when I tell you... Well, see those clouds up in the sky? I can tell you now that we are going to witness the most astonishing electrical storm you have ever seen in your life.'

Sometimes I had the impulse to ring a friend, just when he needed me, and now and then I could tell when a woman was pregnant even before she knew it. At times, I could even correctly determine the sex of the child. If I remembered, I would tell my wife, but we wouldn't take it seriously. Sometimes I would keep it to myself, and when it happened, she couldn't believe I had anticipated it.

But this day, as if inspired by my words, a first flash of light exploded in the sky. Lightning, thunder and fierce wind preceded the most spectacular storm.

Slowly, a feeling of power started growing inside me. I discovered that I could control, although somewhat awkwardly, the direction and range of the lightning, that I could tell the wind which way to blow. I felt as if I were the apprentice conductor of nature's fantastic symphony.

In the meantime, the malignant being outside was twirling, vociferating and convulsing, becoming smaller amidst deafening roars, which we couldn't tell apart from the thunder. The blinding light of the electrical storm, combined with the supernatural glow coming from the globe on our porch, had a lethal effect on it.

I understood it had come looking for me, because somehow it found out that one day I was going to wake from my long sleep, and it had wanted to stop me. What it didn't know was that its very presence caused exactly what it was trying to avoid: Now, an unstoppable power was rushing out of my fingers and my mind, and I concentrated all that energy towards the monster until I reduced it into something smaller than a meek black mouse, who ran away squeaking. It would have been better for it never to have come.

I remembered, centuries in the past, having been the Master of the weather. I remembered being gigantic and magnanimous; images of wars and storms, creation and destruction, birth and death flashed through my mind with astonishing speed. I remembered my name...

Perfundus: 'He who inspires, who endows, who heals, who purifies.'

... and I remembered my crime and the compassion granted. Inside my heart for the first time, I understood what it meant. At long last, I had been given a second chance.

I turned around to find my wife, and I could see her peeking through the half-opened door of the bedroom; I could see both her and my mother, holding hands, beaming at me.

'You won't believe what has just happened,' I said.

'I think we will,' my wife answered.

'No, you don't understand. I suddenly remembered that a long, long time ago—' I began to say, but she interrupted me, as she often did.

'I know, Perfundus. I was there. I tried to save you, but...' her voice trailed off, as her eyes filled with tears.

I looked at her, my companion, my lover, my nemesis, my saviour, my teacher, my disciple. Then I looked at my mother, who was also crying tears of happiness, still holding my wife's hand. I looked again into my wife's eyes and I recognised the transparent, charismatic eyes of The Enlightened. In a dreamlike trance, I noticed for the first time her previously invisible and now magnificent, radiant wings.

And the monster outside? It had been only a test, one of many to come; or perhaps it was what was left of my previous self?

'Come on,' my wife said, extending her free hand towards me. 'We only have a few lifetimes left. There is still much for you to learn...'

And this time, I took her hand.

While my mother served afternoon tea, the world, unaware of my awakening, lay calm ahead of us in the lightness of a new day outside, now completely free of shadows.

Acknowledgements

I would like to acknowledge the wonderful people who have shared and supported my writing journey since I crafted my first poem as a child. Aside from family, I have had an army of champions: partners, teachers, friends, colleagues, fellow writers, mentors, as well as the editors who published my work in their literary journals and anthologies. Some of those works are included here (reprinted with permission) with acknowledgements at the end of each piece.

A big thanks to my best friend Mark for gifting me the title for this anthology, inspired by the *Songs for Suburban Castaways* he wrote many years ago with his cousin Cliff. Mark continues to be my biggest champion, sounding board, and first proofreader.

Thank you to Sally for her meticulous copy-editing and valuable feedback; and to Karen, who worked her red-pen magic over the final draft.

A mention must go to Albert, who often shared his dreams upon waking – back in the days when we were still a couple. Some of the most whimsical became seeds for the stories in Part 3.

Earlier versions of some of the pieces in Part 1 first appeared in my blog, *Midnight Musings*.

'Purple Butterfly', '21 Years', 'The Reluctant Prophet', 'The Day the Master Fell' and 'The Visitor' were originally written and published in Spanish. During translation (which I did myself), they have been substantially rewritten.